Sherlock Holmes and the Masquerade Murders

FRANK THOMAS

*Sherlock Holmes and the
Masquerade Murders*

A DIVISION OF
OTTO PENZLER BOOKS
NEW YORK

Copyright © 1986 by Frank Thomas

Otto Penzler Books, 129 West 56th Street, New York, NY 10019 (Editorial Offices only)

Macmillan Publishing Company, 866 Third Avenue, New York, NY 10022

Maxwell Macmillan Canada, Inc., 1200 Eglinton Avenue East, Suite 200, Don Mills, Ontario M3C 3N1

Macmillan Publishing Company is part of the Maxwell Communication Group of Companies.

Library of Congress Cataloging-in-Publication Data
Thomas, Frank, 1926–
    Sherlock Holmes and the masquerade murders / by Frank Thomas.
        p.   cm.
    ISBN 1-56287-056-4
    1. Holmes, Sherlock (Fictitious character)—Fiction. 2. Private investigators—England—Fiction. I. Title.
PS3570.H56263S48   1994   93-43210   CIP
813'.54—dc20

Otto Penzler Books are available at special discounts for bulk purchases for sales promotions, premiums, fund-raising, or educational use. For details, contact: Special Sales Director, Macmillan Publishing Company, 866 Third Avenue, New York, NY 10022

10   9   8   7   6   5   4   3   2   1

Printed in the United States of America

Introduction

That time, some years back now, when Sherlock Holmes chose to favor me with praise regarding my recountings of his adventures remains imprinted, indelibly, in my memory. He indicated his pleasure that I had not dealt solely with the many *cáuses célèbres* and sensational trials in which he had figured but had frequently drawn upon incidents, trivial in themselves, but good examples of those faculties of deduction and of logical synthesis, which he had made his special province. He added, alas, that even these cases had been embellished when brought to the public eye, and what should have been studies in logic had been degraded into a series of tales. This was a familiar litany from him, and time had prompted me to suspect the truth of his objection to my occasional colorations.

For the past two years Holmes had worked without pause, and there was not one major case in England, or on the Continent, that he had not been involved with in some manner during this period. His fame in police investigatory agencies was worldwide. His reputation was not confined to those circles in which he operated, however, and I like to think that my recorded case histories had been instrumental in making his name a household word. The shadowy silhouette of the man in the deerstalker and inverness captivated the imagination and faith of the common man. If it was rumored that Holmes was on the case, the solution was an accepted fact. My friend pretended he was unaware that he was an international figure and oft stated that his sole interest lay in observation and the scientific application of his methods along with cold logic and reason. In reality, though he might not admit it to himself, the master sleuth was as pleased as punch at the infallibility that surrounded his name. Also, there were beneficial results. 'Tis said that many a mighty knight fell before the name and not the lance of the legendary Sir Lancelot. I know not if the tales of King Arthur and his Round Table are based in fact, but I do know that many a hardened criminal literally threw in the sponge upon learning that Sherlock Holmes was on his trail.

I have selected this particular case to recount to you because it became a *cause célèbre*, though considerable pains were taken to keep it out of the tabloids to no avail. In fact, the sensation-seeking press had some influence on the matter, though in the final reckoning . . . but I get ahead of myself.

This adventure certainly reveals Holmes at the peak of his inventive efficiency when he stood alone and unafraid against the weight of public opinion. It all began . . .

J.H.W.

1
The Message

. . . on an early winter evening. The gloom was thickening fast, as though someone were folding layers of muslin over a bulls-eye lantern. In the semi-darkness the street lamps on Baker Street hissed themselves to life, casting a feeble yellow glow on the scene and deepening the shadows hovering around their wavering pools of light. Then night enveloped the teeming metropolis of six million, and gas jets within the houses up and down the street became firefly pinpricks in a sea of blackness. Now was the time for goblins and ghosts in the minds of fanciful children. Now was the time for the denizens of the half world of the lawless to stir themselves from their haunts in preparation for their illegal doings that were the warp and woof of the fabric that clothed the underworld of London.

Holmes and I had enjoyed an early dinner. There was a cook in the employ of the household by this time, but I frequently wondered if she did more than fetch and carry for our completely unique landlady. Years had not dulled my tastebuds and I could recognize Mrs. Hudson's artistry with pan and skillet.

The sleuth had just brought three problems to a successful conclusion and had been busy during the day updating his case books and files of clippings. I was anticipating those first signs of restlessness and impatience, indications that his ever-active mind was yearning for the challenges and puzzles that were its playground and the cure for the fits of despondency and boredom that Holmes was subject to.

As though divining my train of thought, the world's only consulting detective exhaled a cloud of smoke and broke the silence that had fallen over our sitting room.

"Watson, I've been remiss. You did not see that message delivered just before our repast."

"Why, no. I must have been upstairs."

As my companion of many years rose from the Queen Anne chair and crossed to the desk to extract an envelope from its drawer, I felt of two minds. Holmes drove himself unmercifully and my medical calling prompted me to welcome a break in his feverish activity. There were, in fact, times that I insisted upon it.* Yet inactivity, as previously indicated, plunged him into such moods of black depression that I was almost tempted to invent a case to shake him out of it. Living with an eccentric perfectionist was not all beer and skittles.

Of course, Holmes might merely show me the bill from Sampson and Co. of Oxford Street for those

---

*The Reigate Squires

linen shirts he had purchased at ten shillings apiece, but the way he had brought up the matter suggested that there might be something more exciting afoot.

To my relief, what he handed me had no sinister overtones and was uncomplicated in nature.

My Dear Mr. Holmes:

Forgive this intrusion on your busy schedule.

We have a mutual acquaintance, Claymore Frisbee, who is most laudatory about your accomplishments. I have from time to time performed some service for this gentleman and Inter-Ocean.

At the moment, I seem to be involved in a matter much more suited to your talents than mine. Should you be in your chambers at sevenish this evening, I wonder if I might have a few words with you.

Cordially,

James Wyndhaven

"Hmmm," I said, "requests an interview and puts it rather nicely. Name means nothing to me."

"Nor to me," replied Holmes.

"Well, then, we're rather in the dark until the chap shows up."

"Not completely." Holmes stuffed shag into the clay pipe he frequently used when he adopted the role of contrarian. "I picture a semi-retired individual, therefore not young. A stock appraiser, I'd say. If I miss the mark, I'll wager it won't be by much."

As I passed back the message, delivered by hand I noted, I fear that familiar expression of incredulity spread over my features once more.

"Really, Holmes, from a short and simple communique like that, how could you come to such a conclusion?"

Leaning his arm against the mantle, my friend regarded me with twinkling eyes.

"The magician who gives away his tricks no longer baffles an audience. However, we'll use this as a test for your talents. Study Wyndhaven's message and then reduce it, in your own words, to the shortest possible form."

Accustomed to his seemingly strange requests, I viewed the letter again, determined to do my best.

"Let's see. This was delivered by hand so I'll start with a brief greeting."

S.H.

Arriving around seven. James Wyndhaven.

My questioningly glance at the sleuth was rewarded by a nod and a smile.

"Splendid, Watson."

"Actually, I merely copied the style of those cables you send."

"Touché. Now everything he wrote, outside of the basic reason for his message, which you encapsulated so well, is a clue to the man himself."

"Don't see where we have much to work on," I stated truthfully.

"But we do. An insignificant point, but take the greeting. My Dear Mr. Holmes. That particular form of opening is most used by the Scottish."

"Do tell."

"The first sentence is revealing. It suggests concern regarding the problems of others which, in turn, indicates a man of some tact and breeding.

Next he mentions Claymore Frisbee, a man known to us both. A subtle character reference that, and note that he works in a compliment regarding my work. No fool he. In the third paragraph he comes to what is on his mind."

"You feel that he is semi-retired." My statement was more of a question.

"Observe that he has done something for Frisbee 'from time to time.' Here's something else. He mentions Inter-Ocean but does not call it the Inter-Ocean Trust. Obviously, he knows I have been associated with the bank in my line of work, a fact confirmed by his compliment. All right, Claymore Frisbee is the President of Inter-Ocean Trust and whatever Wyndhaven's activities are, he indicates that his infrequent duties are assigned by Frisbee for Inter-Ocean. Now who would be called in, at intervals, by the President to perform a service for the bank? An appraiser."

"You specified a stock appraiser. Why not real estate?"

"The most common collateral for a bank loan is real estate. To judge its value, they have men on their staff and no need to call in an outsider."

"Jewelry, perhaps?"

"Every lending institution has an arrangement with a reputable jewelry concern to do that kind of work and the same can be said for an art dealer and paintings, etc. No Watson, it would be in the field of stock and securities where Inter-Ocean might need a specialist."

"If you say so, Holmes. So we have a middle aged or older security appraiser occasionally called in by the bank. I'm still vague about your assumption that he is semi-retired."

"Wyndhaven suddenly comes upon a matter which he feels unable to cope with and seeks my help. I doubt if one regularly employed and therefore, income conscious, would accept defeat so quickly. Bank employees seldom admit to a lack of knowledge."

"But this Wyndhaven chap can afford to. Well, that makes sense. A moment, though. How do we know that the man came upon this problem suddenly, as you say?"

"Regard the paper and envelope, Watson."

"Plain, both of them. Good quality paper."

"But plain, indicating that the letter was not typed at Wyndhaven's office for he would have used his own stationery. I picture him at Inter-Ocean, or wherever his work took him when he decided to contact me. Oh, please note that he typed it himself."

"Pray tell, how do you know that?"

"Because the typing is not that of a professional. There are no errors, I'll grant you that, but regard the shading of the letters. Some lighter than others. Not a trained typist with an even touch but, rather, one who has learned by himself and become proficient at it."

"A hunt-and-pecker, you mean."

"Exactly."

"Holmes, as always you amaze me."

"You flatter me, old chap. A bit more conjecture here than I approve of but I feel we have a fair idea of what Mr. Wyndhaven will be like when he arrives around seven. He gave himself a little leeway as regards time, but I'll wager that he won't need it."

"Why?"

"Put that down to a feeling, for it is not based on hard fact. Wyndhaven just strikes me as the type that will appear as the clock tolls the hour."

It was here that the sleuth did miss the mark.

Holmes informed our page boy that we expected a visitor and, close on to the hour of seven, there was a gentle tap at our hall door. Billy ushered in a stout, portly man in a gray suit. As he strode heavily into the room, my eyebrows escalated in surprise, for this was not our potential client but the familiar figure of Inspector Athelney Jones of New Scotland Yard.

"Evening, gents," said the red-faced, burly, and plethoric policeman.

"Ah, Jones," replied my companion smoothly and his eyes caught mine with a signal towards the spirit cabinet. "Do be seated and tell us the latest doings at the Yard, though I should mention that we are expecting someone."

The inspector registered disappointment. "Blast me but that's a comedown, for I hoped you might accompany me on a call. Knowing your fondness for all that's unusual or strange, Mr. Holmes, I'd a mind it's a matter that could be of interest."

"Our visitor may be delayed," replied Holmes quickly, and I knew he hoped James Wyndhaven would be. "Do tell us what brings you to our door."

Jones' small eyes, peering out from between swollen and puffy pouches, swiveled from Holmes to me.

"I'm in hopes Dr. Watson might lend an ear, for he could give an assist and that's a fact."

Busy with tantalus and gasogene, my head jerked up in amazement. Seldom did a visitor to our quarters seek to enlist my aid. Most oft they had to have my presence explained to them.

"Right with you," I stammered; and then negotiated two tumblers into outstretched hands. Sitting on the sofa, I toasted my companions and looked quizzically at the inspector.

If I was of two minds about Holmes' work schedule, Peter Athelney-Jones was a walking contradiction as regards the world's only consulting detective. We had worked with the husky-voiced, heavy-handed inspector in the Sholto matter,* and he had been a part of that historical night when Holmes had captured the infamous John Clay and saved the City and Suburban Bank's thirty thousand gold napoleons.** Full of bluster and bombast, Jones liked to refer to Holmes as "the theorist" and would loudly proclaim that while my friend had set him on the right track on many occasions, it was mostly a matter of luck. Actually, the inspector was in awe of Holmes and in abject fear that someone would realize this. His path in an investigation was usually

---

*The Sign of the Four.
**The Red Headed League.

well marked by a series of blunders, which were made more obvious by the excuses he offered for them. But he was brave and tenacious and when Holmes made a suggestion, he seized upon it gratefully like a dog snatching at a bone.

It was during this period that Scotland Yard outstripped the Sûreté as the foremost official investigating apparatus, and all its officers had to work their way up through the ranks. A hyphenated name suggested a gentleman dilettante, and Jones found it expedient to drop his first name of Peter, hence the rather unusual Athelney Jones.

"It's like this, gents," stated the inspector after downing half his drink. "Young Hopkins phoned into the Yard about this death in the financial district. Apparently it's heart failure, but Hopkins mentioned something that didn't sit right with him and the Commissioner put me on the matter for a second opinion you might say."

"Stanley Hopkins will make his mark," said Holmes with conviction. The young police inspector was rather a protege of the sleuth. "What is it that caught his attention?"

"Well, Sir, the corpse had a history of heart trouble, so that's probably what it amounts to. Hopkins got his wind up because he found nitroglycerine tablets in the man's coat pocket along with. . . ." At this point, Jones consulted his notebook.

". . . a small bottle of amyl nitrate." The inspector turned to me.

"This don't make no sense, Doctor. I don't know

what this amyl stuff is, but I thought nitroglycerine was for blowing things up."

"It sounds like the victim suffered from angina pectoris. A nitroglycerine tablet under the tongue or an inhalation of the fumes of amyl nitrate are the most common methods of providing quick relief from the pain of an attack."

"That explains Stanley Hopkins' suspicions about the matter," exclaimed Holmes.

"It does?" said Jones with a rising inflection.

"You stated the corpse had previous heart problems. Why didn't he take a nitro tablet when he felt an attack coming on?" Holmes thought for a moment and then his eyes rose to mine. "Could he have died immediately, Watson?"

"No. Angina pectoris is a pain in the chest that occurs when the blood supply to the heart muscle is shut off. The pain starts at the top of the breastbone and then shoots down the left arm."

"Then the victim would certainly have time to try to alleviate the attack. This does present points of interest."

Holmes shook his head as though in regret that such a tantalizing puzzle could not be investigated posthaste.

"By the way, who was this unfortunate victim?" he asked, after a moment.

Again Jones referred to his notebook. "Hopkins said he was a securities appraiser named James Wyndhaven."

I almost dropped my drink. Holmes' *sangfroid*

stood him in good stead as he rose and began to divest himself of his purple dressing gown.

"If you don't mind, Jones, Watson and I will go with you. The death may be perfectly normal, as you intimated, but one never knows."

"I thought you was expecting somebody 'round now," said Jones, not sure how he felt about this turn of events having already picked my medical mind.

"I doubt if our visitor is coming," replied Holmes, and there was a grim tone to his voice. "Watson will agree with me, I'm sure."

I did.

2
Three Questions

Jones' carriage took us to our destination in good time. It proved to be the top floor of the Savage Building, well known as the final example of the work of the architect for whom it was named. It was in the offices of Leicester Ltd. that we found Stanley Hopkins. The young policeman was both surprised and delighted when he spied Holmes, for he was a keen student of the methods of the master sleuth. He quickly took us to a small office, indicating the body of a man past middle age, slumped in a desk chair.

"The medical team has been and gone, but I wanted the body to remain until you arrived," he said to Jones.

"Did they give an opinion?" asked the inspector.

"Heart failure."

"Well, Mr. Holmes here seems to go along with your suspicions."

Hopkins exhaled with relief. "I'm grateful for that. We've got enough homicides without my dreaming one up."

Holmes was already viewing the desk and the late

James Wyndhaven, seated behind it, with care. Out came the ever present pocket glass to subject the body to a close scrutiny. The articles on the desk, few in number and standard, then claimed his attention. As he progressed I did not hear those exclamations, which were so frequently a part of one of his meticulous searches for clues. Seemingly, his efforts were not proving very fruitful.

When my friend's attention shifted to the carpet, as I knew it would, I recalled that our locale was well known in financial circles.

Frontnoy Leicester, an old man by now, had found the better mousetrap and exploited it well. Schooled in Cumberwell University of Business, he had left the chair of Professor of Economics at Harcourth College to establish an investment firm. Not one cut from the usual cloth either, for he chose the risky but potentially rewarding path of refusing any account that was not in excess of one hundred thousand pounds. His clients had personalized attention, an unlimited number of conferences with their portfolio managers and were pampered and catered to. A barber was available nearby, and an investor could enjoy a pleasant morning discussing his affairs with his advisor while getting a trim as a relaxing bonus. The old line investment houses made snide remarks about this approach like: "Go to Leicester's and get trimmed," but their ridicule stuck in their craws when the then youthful Leicester embarked on a series of financial coups that suggested access to a crystal ball and an accurate one. There was a popular rush to his doors, for the world, especially the financial world, loves a winner. Leicester used this popularity to further upgrade his client list. He seemed to have the innate ability to recognize greatness in others. No so much in his associates as in the financial giants-to-be. When the late Basil Selkirk* took a position, Leicester money was not far behind. For years he had courted the Selkirk interests to no avail, but it was well known that he did handle the British investments of Manheim of Germany as well as the Dutch diamond syndicate. They laughed when he stayed clear of the Netherlands Sumatra manipulation, but his was the last laugh.

By now, Holmes had dusted off his trousers and was inspecting the tie of the corpse with his glass for the second time. Finally, he turned to his three observers with a gesture that he was done.

"Did you find anything, Mr. Holmes?" Hopkins had been watching the sleuth's every move while Jones had viewed Holmes' inspection with resigned patience.

"Three questions occur," stated the sleuth. "First, what was he working on?"

"Working?" echoed Jones, for want of something better to say.

"The man was an appraiser, was he not?"

Stanley Hopkins nodded.

"Then I would assume that he was here to give his opinion of the value of certain securities. But we

---

*Sherlock Holmes and the Golden Bird.

have no stocks or bonds in evidence or even an indication of notes that Wyndhaven might have taken. The blotter is bare."

"He could have finished his work and been thinking things over," suggested Jones, but this idea didn't sound good, even to him.

"Next," continued Holmes, "what was he afraid of?"

As we stared at him, dumbly, Holmes indicated the face of the corpse.

"Come, come gentlemen; even in death his features reflect terror. It's as if he suddenly saw a coiled cobra on the desk in front of him."

"Well," stated Jones, "I'd be afraid of death."

"Suffering from angina pectoris, he would not necessarily know that he was going to die."

"That was his ailment, Mr. Holmes," exclaimed Hopkins, "for I was able to contact his doctor by phone. His number was in the deceased's billfold. How did you know?"

"We have Watson here to thank for that. He was clued by the nitro tablets and amyl nitrate in the man's pocket. The items that alerted you, Hopkins."

"Right on, Mr. Holmes. From the position of the body, it is obvious that the man made no move to secure either."

"Could he have been prevented from doing that?" asked Jones.

Holmes regarded the Scotland Yard man with approval tinged with surprise.

"Good show, Jones. A possibility; but then

Wyndhaven would have been struggling with his murderer, and neither his position nor expression fits in with that idea. Look at him closely, gentlemen. It's as though he were gazing into the jaws of death."

I shuddered inwardly. "You mentioned a third question."

My friend crossed to behind the desk, pointing at the corpse's tie.

"What about this burn mark on the victim's neckwear? It is certainly recent."

"Dash it, I forgot," exclaimed Hopkins. The youthful inspector laid a half-smoked cigarette on the desk. "When the body was found by the porter, this was lying on the victim's tie, smouldering. The porter removed it when he inspected the body to see if Wyndhaven was dead."

'Hmmmmm. A lit cigarette, which presumably fell from Wyndhaven's lips as he was dying. Being seated at the time, it dropped on his tie."

"That's the way it looked to me, Mr. Holmes," said Hopkins.

Holmes the pragmatist, Holmes the cold theorist, had to have an intuitive sense as well, which he indicated with a searching glance at me.

I certainly had a query for Hopkins. "You spoke to the man's doctor, you said. Did he indicate that Wyndhaven's heart ailment was serious?"

"Yes, Sir. The first attack was five years ago. Dr. Anstruther was not surprised when I told him his patient had died."

"Anstruther, eh? Good man." Sensing Holmes' thought, I gave him an affirmative nod. "The corpse shouldn't have been smoking at all. Knowing Anstruther, he would have forbidden the use of nicotine."

"I was wondering about that," said Holmes with a pleased expression. Even the world's greatest detective likes to have his thoughts corroborated. "Well, gentlemen, those are the questions that come to my mind. I believe answers to them would go a long way towards solving this matter."

"Half a minute," burst out Jones, anxious to become part of the discussion. "We've got this here nitro whatever and cigarette burns, but we've also got a corpse with a history of heart trouble. Couldn't that be what killed him?"

"Indeed it could," agreed Holmes.

"Well, natural causes is the opinion I'm giving the Commissioner."

"But a moment ago, Jones, you advanced the idea of someone forcibly preventing Wyndhaven from securing his medication."

"Because you got me tangled up with all this hypothesis." Jones stumbled over the last word but he got it out. "We've got robberies and knifings and terrorists planting dynamite in the underground, and here we are wasting time on a simple case of heart failure."

"Possibly we should get Hopkins' full story before hazarding an opinion," suggested Holmes.

Jones could find no immediate objection to this, so

he subsided, but his small eyes were sullen. Hopkins was eager to oblige the sleuth.

"I was at Cox and Bancroft, the jewelry firm, making a final report on a smash and grab of last night. I came out on Bayfield Street and noted a constable along with a watchman and porter making fast tracks into the building here, so I tagged along."

"Fortunate that you did," exclaimed Holmes. "Prevented excited amateurs from trampling around the body destroying clues."

"It would seem, Mr. Holmes, from your investigation, that there weren't many clues to be had." Jones had a sly look of satisfaction about him.

"My remark was a generality," exclaimed the sleuth, a caustic bite to his tone. "Pray continue, Hopkins."

"The body was discovered by the porter at quarter of six."

"The office was closed by then?" asked Holmes.

"Yes, Sir. I was able to reach Mr. Frontnoy Leicester by phone. He was suitably upset when I explained the situation and then he requested that I check the door to his private office, which I did. When I assured him that it was locked, he seemed much relieved and said he would make himself available in the morning."

Holmes seemed to find this information of particular interest.

"Hmmmm. That may answer one of my questions. Strange that Leicester didn't rush down here immediately."

There was silence for a moment, broken by Hopkins.

"I did get a rundown on the staff from Mr. Leicester."

"Ah, yes, the others who would have keys to the offices," stated Holmes as he directed a meaningful look at Jones.

"What? The staff? Oh, the staff." Out came the inspector's notebook. Officially, Athelney Jones was conducting the investigation, and he was grateful to make motions confirming this. "Now, who besides Frontnoy Leicester works here?"

"Three account executives—Weems, Andrews, and Macy—one male file clerk, a female receptionist, plus two secretaries, female."

"Who has keys to the offices?"

"The account executives and the receptionist. According to the porter, everyone had gone for the evening."

"Strange," said Holmes, "that they would leave Wyndhaven, not an employee of the firm, alone in the offices."

"I gathered that he was no stranger. He was considered the best independent appraiser in London, even though he was semi-retired."

Holmes could not resist a triumphant look at me when Hopkins came up with this news.

"Mr. Leicester said he was the last to go and he felt no concern leaving Wyndhaven, who said he had just a few more items to check out."

In spite of his dim view of the proceedings, Jones'

curiosity kept sparking questions. "Then Leicester was the last one to see Wyndhaven alive before the porter found him. What was he doing in here, by the way?"

"The porter checks the offices every night after they are vacated. Both he and the night watchman are bonded and have been with the building for twenty years."

"Well, if I really thought that there was any ho-key-pokey going on, and I don't, I'd have the cuffs on Leicester and that porter as well." Jones seemed relieved at having enunciated this thought and given an indication of how a real police investigation should be managed at the same time.

Holmes gazed at the ceiling as if in search of patience from a divine source.

"Jones," he stated, "Frontnoy Leicester may soon be Sir Frontnoy Leicester. He is, as they say, highly connected. The Prince happens to be one of his clients."

Jones' small eyes grew larger and his jaw dropped perceptibly.

"Blimey, Mr. Holmes."

"And the Earl of Portman and others I could name whose aura is more of Buckingham than the Exchange. Handcuffing Leicester could well lead to your checking dark corners of the streets of Soho. Which brings us to an important point." Holmes was ready to elaborate and then checked himself as a thought struck him.

"Hopkins, who was Wyndhaven working for?"

"The Inter-Ocean Trust, Mr. Holmes."

Temporarily subdued, Jones jumped back into the thick of it.

"There now, Mr. Holmes, you can surely get what's to be learned from the Inter-Ocean side of it."

It was generally thought that Sherlock Holmes was on an annual retainer to the bank and insurance complex headed by Claymore Frisbee. This supposition was incorrect. Holmes cherished his freedom to pick and choose cases. This was a sore point with me, for I knew the president of Inter-Ocean had offered the sleuth a princely sum more than once to take charge of all the firm's investigations, but my friend was not to be swayed in this matter.

"It strikes me," said the sleuth, almost to himself, "that this case could well run into roadblocks if old Mr. Leicester chooses to erect them. I'd like to go over this suite of offices now while there's no one here to say us nay."

"Mr. Holmes," said Athelney Jones, "you are a man to be humored, and we all know that you are a connoisseur of crime, but duty is duty and I have gone rather far out in this affair already. Hopkins' sniffer comes up with something stale because of them nitrowhatever. . . ."

"Nitroglycerine tablets," prompted Holmes in an exasperated manner.

"Right, and that amyl stuff. . . ."

"Amyl nitrate," I interjected.

"But facts is what we need. Old Sergeant Mul-

vaney used to pound that into me when I was walking the streets, younger than you, Hopkins. What
are the facts? Here's a man with a faulty pump for
five years. He's alone in this here office. Everybody's
gone. There's a watchman on duty in the lobby and
everybody what comes in has to sign his register, and
no one did, for Hopkins checked that out."

Holmes shot an approving look at his young
protege.

"The corpse looks frightened, I'll give you that,
but he might have been startled by a sudden sound
on the street outside."

Jones was pacing back and forth waving his arms
to help make his points, and he suddenly turned and
leveled an outstretched finger at me.

"Can you swear, Doctor, that this here appraiser,
considering his problem, couldn't have just keeled
over in his chair, the lighted cigarette dangling from
his lips, and died then and there?"

I thought for a moment and then came up with the
only answer possible.

"No, I cannot."

Triumph infiltrated Jones' red face.

"Now the Commissioner told me to come down
here and give the layout a once-over to see if Hopkins' suspicions were warranted. My report, which
I'm givin' him shortly, is death by natural causes."

I felt that, for Jones, that was a rather workman-
like job. At least he wasn't arresting everybody in
sight. Evidently, Holmes agreed with me.

"Well stated, Jones."

"It was?" exclaimed the boisterous protector of the peace, much surprised. Then the bulldog quality of his features softened and he resembled, for a moment, a small boy receiving a high mark from a patient teacher.

"However," continued Holmes quietly, "there is one facet of this matter that you are not privy to. The late Mr. Wyndhaven contacted me prior to his death."

"Did he now," breathed Jones. The decision in his manner drained away, and even the self-contained Hopkins was wide eyed.

"Wyndhaven was the visitor Watson and I were expecting when you arrived."

"Blimey. This puts a different face to the matter."

"Especially since, among other things, Wyndhaven informed me that he had come upon a problem more in my line of work than his. Grant me this supposition. Someone did not want Wyndhaven to arrive at Baker Street at seven this evening. The appraiser had discovered something that a person or persons did not want known."

Jones, now ready to grab on to any suggestion the master sleuth might make, was nodding violently.

"Agreed, Mr. Holmes, but what do I tell the Commissioner?"

"Simply that, in your opinion, there is sufficient reason to keep the books open on this matter. You do not advocate, at this time, that the Yard take a definitive position on how James Wyndhaven met his death."

The inspector's notebook appeared rapidly. "I
say, Mr. Holmes, that's a real sharp way of puttin'
it. Hope you don't mind if I make a note of them
words." Scribbling hastily, Jones placed himself on
the Holmes team, as 'twere. "What was it you had
in mind for us to do while we've got the run of the
place, so to say?"

"Giving the rest of this emporium of high finance
a looking at. Where is the porter, Hopkins?"

"By the lift, Sir, where I left him with the
constable."

"And you have his master keys?"

"Yes, Sir."

"Well and good. Gentlemen. . . ." Sherlock
Holmes indicated the door to the office in which we
had found Wyndhaven, and we filed out.

The suite of offices that housed Leicester Ltd.
occupied the entire top floor of the Savage Building.
Each of the three account executives had his domain,
which we inspected, but the lair of the lion, Frontnoy Leicester, resisted the master keys. Evidently its
impressive door, when locked, could only be opened
by Leicester himself. There was a room containing
nothing but steel filing cabinets and a large area
next to the reception room where the secretaries and
the file clerk plied their trade.

The ceilings throughout were high and artificial
light was provided by striking chandeliers. I was not
surprised at the luxuriance of the surroundings.
Leicester had broken into a highly competitive field
with a splash and obviously believed in a corporate

image that reeked of what his clients were most interested in—money.

The prize exhibit was the conference room. Its long table was polished to a mirror-like sheen, and there were fully a dozen chairs running its length. I could imagine one of the firm's most important clients, like the steel tycoon Manheim, being ushered into this stately room to find the entire personnel of Leicester Ltd. in attendance, just to be of service to his account. There was a long running bar against one wall that could have easily accommodated the overflow from the Criterion on a busy day. Suddenly my lips twitched with mirth as a picture came to my mind. One of Holmes' close associates, the American "Get Rich Quick" Wallingford, belonged here. Known as the King of the Confidence Men, he now worked with Holmes when needed and also acted as part of that intricate apparatus constructed by the sleuth's older brother, Mycroft Holmes, the second most powerful man in England. I could just picture Wallingford using a room like this in the manner of a leading tenor using a Graustark backdrop. In it he would be able to sell almost anyone on almost anything. Sand for the Sahara, perhaps? Not beyond Wallingford's ability at all.

I noted puzzlement in both Jones' and Hopkins' eyes when, in each room that we subjected to a cursory inspection, Sherlock Holmes paced off the length and breadth. This was something my friend did almost automatically, for he could govern his stride to an exact three feet, and when he left I well knew that he could tell you the dimensions of each room with remarkable accuracy. The sleuth had found this habit of his of help in the past and would, no doubt, in the future as well.

Finally, Holmes was satisfied. At the archway leading to the reception area, he indicated the office containing the unfortunate James Wyndhaven.

"No reason not to have the body removed now, is there?"

"I'll get the constable on it right away, Mr. Holmes," said Hopkins.

As the youthful inspector headed towards the lift, Jones sidled alongside Holmes in a surreptitious manner, looking for all the world like a race track tout with a hot tip.

"I'll take care of the Commissioner, Mr. Holmes. You'll check this out on the Inter-Ocean side, right?"

"Right," said Holmes in a conspiratorial tone, for he dearly loved his little jokes.

"We'll get to the bottom of this, Sir," whispered Jones, "and what a story it will be. Man ostensibly dies of heart attack, but alert police work uncovers murder. Investigation reaches into high places."

Jones paused with a beatific smile on his face, and then his expression sobered. "I'm goin' to have a word with the porter. Just maybe there's something he forgot to tell Hopkins."

As we followed our new ally, Holmes was having difficulties suppressing the mirth that was welling up within him.

"Watson, the possibility of error is always with us. If Wyndhaven did not meet with foul play, we will never hear the end of it from Athelney Jones; and that is a fact that would even be acceptable to that mentor of Jones' youth, the somewhat legendary Sergeant Mulvaney."

3

The Singular Solicitor

There had been rain in the late night and early morning which lulled me into sound sleep. Globules of moisture propelled, confetti-like, by the north wind against the glass of my window had a soothing effect, and the warmth of my blankets and softness of my down bolster were made more appealing by the subconscious thought that I was not having to brave the cold and wetness without.

When I finally stirred at a late hour, I made a creaky descent to our sitting room, favoring my old wound from the Afghan War, which invariably reminded me of my military days when the weather turned foul. However, breakfast and a bit of moving around and I felt I would be fiddle fit.

Holmes, who had finished his morning repast, rang for Mrs. Hudson as I found my way to my chair at the table.

"Let me pour you some of this excellent coffee, old chap," he said, crossing to the great silver urn with the candle beneath it which was seldom empty. "Here you are. Two lumps, of course. Now you can awaken your brain by reading of the events of last night."

I choked on my first sip. "The Wyndhaven matter has made the journals?"

"Most assuredly. I deduce that the reporter majored in romantic literature, but see for yourself." He indicated a story in *The Morning Beacon*.

Well-Known Consultant Dies

Last evening, James Wyndhaven, financial appraiser, breathed his last. Victim of a serious heart ailment, he was assumed by one eyewitness to have died of his affliction. Your reporter is intrigued by the amount of official activity in connection with this matter. Part is due to coincidence since Stanley Hopkins, rising young Scotland Yard inspector, was in the area in connection with another case and immediately took charge of the Wyndhaven investigation. As an indication of the efficiency and dedication of our detective police force, Inspector Athelney Jones, veteran of many a notorious case, was dispatched to join his young colleague. A considerable period of time elapsed before the body of the unfortunate man was removed from the offices of a leading financial house.

My eyes rose from the paper to Holmes, who was re-reading the article over my shoulder. "I see Frontnoy Leicester's influence kept the name of his establishment out of print."

"And saved himself the inconvenience of morbid thrill seekers as well as the fourth estate. More than we can boast."

"What?"

"Finish it, old chap, and I'll clue you to the latest."

I resumed my reading with added interest.

At Scotland Yard, Inspector Jones was prevailed upon to make a statement saying: "In my opinion there is sufficient reason to keep the books open on this matter." When pressed further, the Inspector added: "I do not advocate, at this time, that the Yard take a definitive position on how James Wyndhaven met his death."

"Good heavens, Holmes, he parrotted your words exactly."

"Words meant for the Commissioner and not the sensation-seeking press."

My eyes flew back to the article.

To add to the complexities, Mr. Sherlock Holmes, the world's leading criminologist, was closeted with Inspectors Hopkins and Jones at the scene of death. We are informed on good authority that James Wyndhaven had been in contact with Holmes prior to his unfortunate demise. Mark my words, readers, there is more to this than meets the eye, and *The Morning Beacon* will spare no pains in keeping you informed of developments.

As I lowered the paper, Holmes was lighting up his cherrywood.

"I must learn what reporter wrote that story and avoid him. So far this morning we have had four representatives of other journals at our door, all firmly repulsed by Mrs. Hudson."

At that moment, we heard the knocker at the outer portal of 221B Baker Street.

"More reporters, no doubt," I said.

"Or Claymore Frisbee. I had a few words with him this morning but caught him at a bad time. He volunteered to come here, if business permits. If not, we have an invitation to lunch with him at Simpsons."

By now our dedicated Billy was at the hall door with a card upon a tray.

"Mr. Filbrick Straithway to see you sir," said the page boy. "Says it's about the estate of a Mr. Wyndhaven."

Holmes glanced at the card with raised eyebrows, then dropped it on our desk. "A member of the legal profession, always in evidence when death strikes. All right Billy, show him up. This seems the season for unexpected visitors, does it not, Watson?"

Straithway was tall and thin with iron-gray hair, a complexion so sallow as to be almost yellow and a black moustache that just might have been touched up with some dye. The solicitor's symbol—a briefcase—was with him and he placed it, along with his gloves and walking stick, on our side-table. After greetings, he sat himself carefully in our visitor's chair as if wary of loose springs and adjusted his trousers to preserve their knife-edge crease. I had the feeling he was going to read a will or possibly bring suit against Holmes, myself and Billy. Why Mrs. Hudson was excluded from this fantasy, I cannot say.

Leaning against the desk, Holmes indicated the man's business card.

"You say you represent the estate of the late James Wyndhaven, Mr. Straithway?"

"His heirs actually. My client . . . er . . . former

client was a widower with two offspring. A son, of age of course, and a married daughter who lives in Croydon. I have been in contact with them, a matter made the simpler by their both living in the greater London area. Singularly, they were both very anxious to know one thing. Did James Wyndhaven reveal anything to you before he died?"

Not for the first time, Holmes answered a question with a question.

"Do you or the heirs know what Mr. Wyndhaven was working on?"

The lawyer permitted himself a small smile, in a manner that suggested his facial muscles did not move with ease.

"Mr. Wyndhaven was going over some securities at Leicester Ltd. for the Inter-Ocean Trust. Rather a matter of form you know, since anything handled by Leicester would be top drawer."

"Then why an appraisal?" asked Holmes.

Straithway shrugged. "The Inter-Ocean Trust could be considering a loan to someone who is a friend or associate of one of Leicester's clients. The securities at the investment house being pledged as back-up collateral in the loan application. A matter of good will, mostly. Not at all uncommon."

Now it was Holmes who smiled. "You certainly know more than the newspapers, Mr. Straithway."

"In my position, I would figure to."

After a pause, Straithway nudged Holmes verbally.

"Regarding Wyndhaven. . . ."

"When Watson and I arrived on the scene, the man was already dead."

"Of course. I mean prior to that."

"What James Wyndhaven may or may not have informed me of, I regard as privileged information."

"But the man is dead!"

I was glad that Straithway's attention was concentrated on the sleuth, for my jaw had dropped and my face must have revealed what was going through my mind, namely: "What kind of a charade is this?"

"A client is a client," said Holmes, using his hands expressively.

My friend had not uttered one word that was untrue, but he was laying a false trail as wide as a city block.

"Would not your client's interests be best served through his children? His sole heirs, by the way."

"Obviously they are not my clients."

Straithway was having difficulty concealing his exasperation.

"Mr. Holmes, let me put it to you this way. Will you undertake to represent the interest of the heirs of James Wyndhaven in this matter?" I can assure you that your fees could be considerable . . . along with reasonable expenses, of course."

"Of course." For a moment I thought Straithway's frozen face would brighten, but Holmes' next words deepened his gloom.

"I make a practice of never accepting a case without meeting the principals."

Well, I thought, he's stretched it a bit there. We

certainly were involved in the affair of that cursed Baskerville Hound through the good offices of Dr. Mortimer before meeting Sir Henry Baskerville. Then I corrected myself, for Holmes did not definitely commit himself to the matter until Mortimer brought Sir Henry to our quarters.

The lawyer began an objection, but Holmes overrode him.

"You might well contend that I would be acting for the estate, and I'm sure that you enjoy the complete confidence of your clients as well as a carte blanche regarding arrangements."

"My words exactly, Sir."

"I still consider the corpse to be my client while the matter about which he contacted me remains unresolved."

"It was only a letter," I thought to myself, "and not a revealing one at that."

"In plain words, Mr. Holmes, you will not tell me what James Wyndhaven told you prior to his demise?"

A distinct chill had settled over the discussion.

"No, Sir, I will not."

Straithway rose with a shrug, collecting his briefcase, gloves and hat. "Then I am frittering away both our time. Good day, gentlemen."

As the lawyer made for our hall door, it opened most conveniently and I wondered if Billy had had his ear to panel or eye to keyhole.

I could barely wait for the footsteps of our visitor to fade away before confronting Holmes.

"What was that all about?"

"An impression, old chap, prompted by a zealous reporter who printed everything he could learn. Refer to the Beacon article. He mentions an eyewitness. Obviously he got to the porter. Then he hied himself to the Yard and collared our wordy friend, Athelney Jones, always on the lookout for a beneficial story in the journals. Jones eagerly spilled all he knew, but he did not know all. I informed the inspector, to prevent his trying to close the case, that Wyndhaven had contacted me prior to his death."

"Which was the truth," I exclaimed.

"I didn't feel called upon to tell Jones that the contact had been a letter requesting an appointment. What need of that? When Jones relayed this information to his reporter friend, it came out in the following manner." Holmes read from the Beacon, " 'We are informed on good authority that James Wyndhaven had been in contact with Holmes prior to his unfortunate demise.' "

"What is your point?"

"That anyone reading this article might well think that Wyndhaven had spoken to me . . . us."

"As did Straithway."

"Which suggests an interesting possibility. Someone was sufficiently concerned about what Wyndhaven had learned to do him in. Would not the same person or persons be very worried about how much Sherlock Holmes and Dr. Watson know of the matter?"

I was staring goggle-eyed at my friend when the

door opened and Mrs. Hudson appeared with my belated breakfast. After she had clucked about, gotten everything arranged, and departed, I found my voice.

"I say, Holmes, you are stretching it, for that is pure conjecture."

"It is?" Then how about our visitor, Filbrick Straithway? I mentioned having a few words with Claymore Frisbee this morning. They included his asking me if I knew James Wyndhaven personally. On learning that I did not, he seemed much surprised and said: 'Oh, I thought two perennial bachelors like you chaps would have run into each other somewhere.' "

"Perennial bachelors? You mean. . . ."

"I mean Wyndhaven did not have a son and daughter, and Straithway does not represent his estate. The gentleman, a misnomer no doubt, came here to try and find out what we had learned from Wyndhaven. That is why you were confused as I implanted in his mind the idea that we might, indeed, possess the information that someone is so fearful of. For that reason, Watson, I suggest that you keep handy that awesome piece of ordinance which you came into possession of, for we might well be targets as of now."

Knife and fork in hand, I sat ignoring my breakfast as Holmes' words sank in. The sleuth consulted his watch.

"It's too late for Frisbee to come here, so we'll be lunching with him at half past twelve." He then regarded me and burst out in a peal of laughter, something he did more often than people realized.

"My dear chap, don't let the prospect of an imminent luncheon dull your appreciation of Mrs. Hudson's efforts. If you do not consume those delectable eggs and devour that crisp bacon to the last rasher, it will ruin her morale completely."

It was not luncheon at Simpsons with Claymore Frisbee that had caused me to lose my appetite.

4

The Ghost of the Gunfighter

Holmes, having already been out and about, seated himself by the window as I did my best with breakfast and then scurried upstairs to dress. At least that was my intent, but then I fell prey to a hunch that would not be denied. Hastily I scribbled some lines on a sheet of foolscap. Folding the message, I went down the front stairs and gave it to Billy, with instructions. I wasn't worried about Holmes hearing me, knowing he would remain as I had left him, using the time for intense mental concentration, weighing every particle of evidence to decide which points were essential and which immaterial.

Shaved and bathed, I selected a gray tweed because it dated back a bit when I weighed more than I did now. My need was a loose-fitting coat. Holmes had mentioned potential danger. If armed, he would bypass that ridiculous single-shot salon piece with which he amused himself on occasion and take the Ely 32. Its short barrel allowed it to rest, unnoticed, in a side pocket. I had more to contend with.

Dressed, I opened the drawer to my nightstand and reverently removed the oil-cloth wrappings from my talisman, the golden gun. It had been given to me by the man who had saved my life and Holmes' on that fateful afternoon in Sussex not so long ago.*

He was the greatest marksman I have ever seen and no one could match the blazing speed of Ledger. Little did I realize the legacy that came my way that day in Sussex. Holmes did not know, nor would he have believed me had I told him, for my friend was a creature of fact and cold logic, rightly called the greatest mind in England. The concept of the golden gun would have eluded him completely. You may mark me for a madman, but I knew now that the gun and Ledger had ridden the outlaw trails so long that the colt had become an extension of the man. When forced to use this weapon that Holmes had described, unwittingly but well, as awesome, I was not in control. The gun took charge. I had once shown it to Wells, the closemouthed firearms expert and pride of Her Majesty's Special Branch. Holmes contended that Wells was surely on a par with the German, Von Herter, that blind mechanic who worked wonders for the infamous Professor Moriarty and had joined his late master in the beyond. Wells had given the revolver a long look and then given me an even longer one.

"Where in the name of all that is holy did you

---

*Sherlock Holmes and the Treasure Train.

come by this, Dr. Watson? 'Tis a hair-triggered masterpiece, crafted like nothing I've ever seen."

I would not let Wells inspect the weapon further for, somehow, it seemed a breach of faith. It came from a living legend whom I'd known but a short time but who proved to be a real friend. Perhaps Ledger knew when he gave me this metallic object with a life of its own.

If I carry on like this, I'll sound like naught but a middle aged and portly general practitioner suffering from advanced senility who should be having no association with a weapon of destiny.

My talisman felt cold but comforting against my stomach and upper thigh, and there was no telltale bulge in my coat. The golden gun was ready for whatever danger might threaten.

In our sitting room, the figure of Holmes might as well have been the wax model by the Frenchman Tavernier, which we had used to such good effect on occasion. Seating myself silently, I tried to divert my mind with the latest *Lancet Magazine* to no use. Holmes was consistently casual relative to an accident by intent, as though he were a character in a Nordic opera wearing a cape of invulnerability. I was not wedded to this approach. The picture, which the sleuth had drawn for me, revealed potential problems of an immediate nature, and I wondered if I could aid my friend should a critical moment occur.

Because I was listening for it, I detected the opening and closing of the downstairs door and breathed a sigh of relief when there were no footfalls on the steps leading upwards. Evidently, Billy had been successful in following the instructions that I had given him.

Sometime thereafter, the alarm bell in Holmes' brain must have sounded and he aroused himself from deep contemplation to rise and take note of me.

"Ah Watson . . . and ready I see. You are developing a cat-like lightness of foot. Well, 'tis a mite early, but let us be off to learn what Claymore Frisbee can tell us about this tangled skein."

On our threshold, I was surprised to see a closed carriage waiting at the curb. There were usually conveniences available, there being a stand just up the street by the underground station, but the cabby was none other than Phineas Portney, Holmes' favorite driver.

"Phineas picked me up at the Inter-Ocean Trust this morning, and I told him we might need him around this time," explained Holmes.

Portney knew every by-way of London as well as or better than Holmes, for we had never given him an address that stumped him.

The battered "topper" and frayed velvet on his weathered coat bespoke a faded gentility which came his way via church sales. Phineas liked to dress the part as best he could, though his nose was sufficient as an attention getter, being oversized, veined and alarmingly red. Holmes attributed its hue, accurately, to a working knowledge of all brands of liquid spirits.

The carriage door was opened for us by our singular cabby who seemed in a remarkably cheerful frame of mind for a drinking man, considering the hour. I suspected that the bottle which rested on his bald pate, secured by the tight-fitting topper, had already seen usage.

Phineas knew our destination. After a somewhat overjovial greeting, his whip flicked like summer lightning and the spavined mare, with her tattered straw bonnet, moved slowly away from the curb and then accelerated to a good rate. The mare could show a surprising burst of early foot if called upon, as I had good cause to remember.

Holmes leaned back with his legs outstretched, still going over things in his mind to my way of thinking. There was a silence interspersed with vague street sounds and the clatter of iron-tyred wheels on cobblestones.

A vigorous hammering on the hatch in the ceiling of our carriage snapped me from a temporary lethargy as Portney's hoarse voice rang out.

"Alert! Alert down there! Somethin's awry."

Acting instinctively, I hopped up and balanced myself on the seat, shoving the hatch cover aside and my upper body through the opening. Phineas Portney was urging the mare to draw on her speed as he gestured behind us with his left arm. There was a four wheeler with two horses overhauling us rapidly, of itself no cause for fright. However, in the open window of the conveyance was a man with a Mauser automatic, fitted with a ѕkeletal stock adjusted to his shoulder and an elongated barrel. Through my mind flashed the word "marksman." This elaborate gun was long ranged, firing a small bullet with tremendous velocity. Those who used such a weapon aimed at vital targets.*

Suddenly the entire scene froze. The man with the Mauser in the carriage bearing down upon us and its rascally looking driver whipping his team were like figures in a mural painted upon a wall. Superimposed, in my mind's eye, was that hilltop in Sussex with the afternoon sun behind it, silhouetting three figures with Smith-Enfield rifles trained on Holmes, myself and Ledger. In a blur, Ledger's hand disappeared under his coat and reappeared firing the Colt with the parrot beak handle and the golden barrel. There was a continuous drumbeat of sound as five shots went off in one and one-fifth of a second, and the three figures atop the hill were dead before their bodies hit the ground.

Then the tableau was erased by the roaring of the gun somehow in my hand. The man in the carriage window stared stupidly at empty fingers, for the Mauser was blown away. The hat atop the driver disappeared. Then the connection pin holding the carriage to the team was smashed. The plunging horses were loose and galloping down the street,

---

*In the Spanish-American War, U.S. forces faced the Mauser, purchased by the Spaniards who, at that time, were not greatly involved in the manufacture of weaponry. Non-fatal wounds healed with remarkable speed since the velocity of the bullet inflicted a small hole. In contrast, the Colt .45, developed during the Morro Rebellion, firing a soft-nosed bullet, carves a veritable tunnel upon impact.

dragging their driver, his fingers frozen on the reins
with fear, after them. There was a flash of metal in
the hand of the second man within the carriage and,
of a sudden, he screamed as blood spurted from his
wrist. There was a fifth shot, but I knew not where it
went—not until a body slowly slid from the second-
story window of an empty house along the route and
fell with gathering speed to the ground. The out-of-
control carriage crashed into a street lamp, which it
demolished. A rifle had fallen with the body, and it
went off, shattering the remnants of glass in a window of the deserted building.

Two constables charging up the street managed to
halt the runaway team whose driver had finally relin-
quished the reins. His body was supine on the cobblestones, a mass of lacerations and contusions. The sight
of London's finest told me that my message to Mac-
Donald at the Yard had been heeded. One of the officers
approached our vehicle, now drawn to a halt.

"An attempted ambush if I ever seen one, Doctor.
Help is on its way, and we'll have the cuffs on the lot
of 'em."

Suddenly there was silence broken by the groans
of the wounded man in the carriage. His companion
descended from it of his own accord, still looking
stupidly at his empty hands as if in search of the
intricate Mauser gun.

"Plain case of shock," I thought.

Holmes was on the street, Ely revolver in hand,
alert for further danger, but there was no need. The
golden gun had done the job.

When the police wagon arrived with reinforcements, it was time for our luncheon engagement. Holmes had words with the officer in charge, and we departed for Simpsons. I noticed Phineas Portney carefully replacing his topper and wiping his lips. I rather wished that he had asked me to join him.

As we completed our trip, Holmes gave me several sideways glances and then articulated his thoughts.

"In times gone by, old chap, I never saw you in action save when we chased that steam launch, the Aurora, down the Thames after the Agra Treasure. But in the past year, you have given two demonstrations of the fanciest shooting I've ever seen."

"You forget Ledger."

"Oh, well, he was unique. No doubt about that. Tell me, how did you spot that chap in the window? The Sergeant told me you caught him right between the eyes. Considering the distance, that's uncanny."

"It was all so fast, Holmes," I said truthfully, "and it was a bit of a sticky wicket. Charge it to instinct—good fortune—what have you."

"If instinct, dear fellow, I'm more than glad you chose the field of medicine and we joined forces. I rather shudder at the thought of facing you in the O.K. Corral or some such locale." He shook his head rapidly as though in disbelief. "Dash it but it's puzzling, and that's a fact."

I was eager to let the matter drop, which it did. Holmes fell silent trying to assess the happening in his mind. I wished that he could do it for me. Then, like the vista of a tranquil lake to a thirsty desert traveler, an illogical solution to an impossible series of events teased my thoughts. I knew it was but a mirage, but what other explanation was there? "Could Ledger," I wondered, "have died on some distant shore and I have become the medium that can bring back the ghost of the gunfighter?"

5
Luncheon at Simpsons

As it happened, Claymore Frisbee was a trifle late, so our arrival at Simpsons coincided with his. When we were seated, Holmes suggested that recent events called for a libation. Frisbee looked a mite surprised but agreed, ordering a whiskey and water, as did Holmes. I requested mine straight, in desperate hopes that my hand would remain steady when I downed it. Evidently, Simpsons served others who experienced nervous problems at lunchtime, for our waiter brought my drink in an oversized shot glass. I downed it abruptly, which drew another surprised look from our banker friend, but he had more important things on his mind.

"About this Wyndhaven matter, Holmes. As you know, he was working for me when it happened. Like others, I thought he had fallen prey to his trick heart, but now there is doubt. What is the real story?"

Holmes chose his words carefully. "There is reason to suspect that he met with foul play." Then his stern features relaxed into a wry smile. "Good heavens, I sound like that reporter on the Beacon."

"I read the story, of course. It would seem all of
London did. Now I know your style, Holmes. All I
want is an opinion, and I won't hold you to it. Was
Wyndhaven done in?"

"I think so."

The banker's palm slapped the table in front of
him. "That tears it. He was an employee of Inter-
Ocean at the time, which has some bearing. More
important, he was a friend. We rather started out
together, you see. Wyndhaven could have gone further had he wished. He had an aversion to regular
hours and rather liked doing things his own way. He
did well, you understand, but was of a free-lance
disposition, not a conformist."

Frisbee paused and took a second sip of his drink
as though in memory.

"Would you," continued the banker, "investigate
his death on my behalf. Nothing to do with the bank,
though I know some chaps who would gladly con-
tribute to a war chest. Let's consider the fee to be of
your choosing."

This was a handsome offer and Holmes accepted
it.

The vivid memory of our so recent escapade was
nudged aside slightly by a warm glow brought on by
the realization that friendship was not just a word in
our society.

After we had ordered, Frisbee, who knew his
man, got to the case in a manner that must have
pleased Holmes.

"Being close with Wyndhaven for so long, what can I reveal that would help you? Enemies . . . I can't think of any. Nor of anyone who suffered a bad turn because of his work. Certainly not in connection with Inter-Ocean. If there had been a financial scandal that he helped uncover, I would have heard of it."

"Agreed," replied Holmes. "Am I correct in thinking that Wyndhaven was checking the portfolio of a Leicester client in connection with a loan you might make?"

"I see I'm not the first you've approached about this."

"But you are."

"How, then, did you know that?"

"One Filbrick Straithway, solicitor, told me. Does the name mean anything?"

"No."

"Didn't think it would. In fact, I think it only exists on a spurious business card. However, he does represent someone or is fronting for them. Someone deeply interested in what Wyndhaven discovered. Whose portfolio was the deceased checking?"

Frisbee almost laughed. "Manheim's, the German steel tycoon. Forgive my seeming to treat this lightly, but Inter-Ocean has no concern about the assets of Herr Manheim. The appraisal had to be made, for it is part of our procedure, and any other bank's as well. I gave the job to Windy . . . er, Wyndhaven, but it wasn't anything that demanded his expertise. In the popular parlance, 'I shoved him a fee.' "

"You mention his expertise. What was it that made him good at what he did?"

"Counterfeits were his speciality. Securities are presented to the bank as collateral or, say, as part of a business entity that the bank is putting together. Some of them might not be the real thing."

"A moment," I said. "I thought it was currency that involved counterfeit plates."

The banker smiled, a little grimly. "Anything that can be printed legally, Doctor, can be duplicated illegally. The trick is that the duplication is not perfect, and Wyndhaven was a rare bird when it came to spotting the bogus; be it stock, bonds, certificates of ownership or, as you mentioned, money. I used to tell him he could smell the queer."

Noting my confusion, he explained.

"An American expression. It means counterfeit, illegal printing."

"I know Herr Manheim," stated Holmes, flashing me a quick look.

Of course, I well remembered our connection with the German tycoon, relative to the Sacred Sword matter.

"Do you really?" exclaimed Frisbee.

"The obvious has already occurred to all of us," continued Holmes. "How could a counterfeit be in the possession of a man like that? Ignoring whatever may be in his portfolio at Leicester's, the art objects belonging to him that are on display in this country alone would underwrite most of the loans you have on the Inter-Ocean books."

"And then some," agreed Frisbee.

"We seem to have reached a impasse," I stated, then wished I'd remained silent. The words had a pontific air.

"What is your conclusion, Holmes?" asked Frisbee.

"A temporary one. Let's say a working hypothesis. Wyndhaven discovered something not necessarily relative to Manheim."

Our discussion was interrupted at this point, by none other than the commissioner of police.

Cecil Brickstone was passing our table with two men whom I did not know when he caught sight of Holmes. After a word to his companions, the commissioner approached us.

"I say, Holmes, this is fortunate."

"How do you do, Commissioner. You know . . ."

"Watson? Of course?"

"And this is . . ."

"Claymore Frisbee, naturally." Brickstone's hand rested on the banker's shoulder. "Dropping off at the club this evening?"

"Expect to."

"Billiards at eight?"

"Delighted."

Social amenities disposed of, Brickstone centered on Holmes again and lowered his voice.

"Wanted a word with you, Holmes. This Wyndhaven thing."

Tables are comfortably separated at Simpsons but, with the arrival of the police commissioner, two men adjacent to us began to lean in our direction, their ears cocked. Brickstone was far from dull, and an expression of annoyance fled across his face.

"Hardly, the place, obviously. My office? Ten tomorrow?"

"Agreed," said Holmes, and that was that.

The commissioner rejoined his guests, or hosts for all I knew, and Holmes and I exchanged thoughtful looks with Claymore Frisbee.

"What have we here?" asked the banker.

"Disquietude in high places," replied the sleuth. "The very well-connected Frontnoy Leicester would be much pleased if your old friend had died without complications. I anticipated his making some waves to have the official verdict read that way, and he's wasted no time."

"He wouldn't. This will present difficulties?"

"Not insoluble. Even if the Commissioner rams through 'death by natural causes,' I'll stay on the case. The difficulty is proving I'm right."

Two waiters and the maitre d'hotel arrived with our order and a wine list, declined by my companions but accepted by me. On their departure, Holmes continued.

"We may just be singing up the wind, you know. I have not seen the autopsy report, but I can discuss that with the Commissioner."

"That could be what Brickstone has in mind," I said, looking at the brighter side.

Holmes nodded. "Or he may have already received a report on our near fatal street encounter."

"Your what?" asked Frisbee.

"An elaborate attempt was made on our lives less than an hour ago."

After a stunned moment, the banker recovered with a thought.

"Holmes, surely that is proof positive that your theory regarding Wyndhaven is correct."

"To us, yes. But were I arguing at Old Bailey for the heart failure cause, I would attribute the attack to enemies from the past. Remnants of the Moriarty apparatus or some of Baron Dowson's gang."

Frisbee pressed more wine upon me and ordered a glass for himself.

"By jove! Right on the street you say? What happened?"

"I'm not all that sure myself." The imp of merriment took possession of Holmes' eyes. "My indispensable associate, that famous marksman, Dr. John Watson, took charge of the affair. Though he is attempting to look modest at the moment, let me assure you that he was a blend of 'China' Gordon and Wyatt Earp."

Frisbee didn't quite know how to take this, but he did not press the matter.

"Thank heavens you are both unscathed."

"Not so the opposition." There was satisfaction in Holmes' manner. "One fatality, one wounded, another badly cut and bruised, and a fourth reduced to a state of shock."

"Good heavens, it sounds like a small-scale war."

"The authorities will be able to identify our assailants, though I doubt if that will prove helpful. They bore the mark of hired mercenaries. Probably not aware of who was really paying the bill."

"Arranged through an intermediary you think?" In spite of himself, the banker exhibited a morbid fascination as though caught up by a melodrama at the Savoy Theatre.

"Our ersatz solicitor, Filbrick Straithway, rather fits that part," said Holmes, but his mind was elsewhere. "Back to Wyndhaven's being at Leicester Ltd. It is probably of no import, but what is the loan at your bank that is involved?"

"A German optical firm planning to open a London outlet. Their credit rating is good, but all their collateral is on the continent. To expedite matters, their representative, Johannes Schmitz by name, stated that the project had the blessings of Manheim and that he would speak for the loan."

Both Holmes and I adopted a quizzical look, prompting Frisbee to enlarge on this.

"Manheim was agreeable to guaranteeing the loan. That in itself should have settled the issue, but there is always some hair-splitter on our board of directors. The simplest way to assure our people that Manheim had sufficient funds available here in England was an appraisal of his portfolio at Leicester's. In this case needless, but not all of our loans have the backing of one of the world's wealthiest men."

"Not a time-consuming task?"

"Far from it. I did not figure in the arrangements,

but I can tell you what transpired. The matter was explained to Leicester, or one of his assistants. An authorization was secured from Manheim's offices in Berlin. A time was agreed upon and Wyndhaven appeared at Leicester's. They would assign him an office, for the contents of an account box is not bandied about and available for passing eyes."

"Box?" I asked.

"Each client of the investment house is assigned a large metal box in which their holdings are kept."

"Like a safety deposit arrangement."

"Exactly, Doctor. The Manheim box would be brought to Wyndhaven. He would take the first security, spread it on the desk top and read it. Then he would make a notation as to title, face value, and his estimate of its worth on the present market."

"Good heavens," I said, "the fellow had to carry the current values of the entire securities listings in his mind."

"The job requires a specialist," conceded Frisbee. "Then Wyndhaven would go through his bag of tricks to be sure that what he held was bona fide."

"What did that entail?" I realized that I was intruding on Holmes' province, but my friend did not indicate displeasure.

"Really don't know the whole of it; not my line you see. I do know that he was particularly sensitive to the feel of whatever he was examining, especially as regards notes. The composition of the paper that currency is printed on is a closely guarded secret. You could blindfold Wyndhaven and he would pick a counterfeit out of a stack of bills just by rubbing it between his thumb and forefinger."

The banker and I both looked at Holmes questioningly.

"Unfortunately, none of this alleviates a trouble spot in my mind. If we assume Wyndhaven died while working on his assignment, where was the Manheim file? Where were his notes? I assume he made some."

"They weren't there?"

When Holmes shook his head, the banker seemed nonplussed.

"This is incredible. We're talking about the port-folio of the firm's most important and influential client. Also, Wyndhaven would have taken notes— depend on it."

Holmes started to make a comment, but Frisbee continued.

"The Manheim file is in the offices right now."

"Why?"

"If it wasn't, Leicester would be making very loud noises to the authorities."

"When notified, he did not even come to his place of business."

"Then he knew where the tycoon's file was."

Holmes' eyes found mine. "That explains Leicester's asking young Hopkins if his private office was locked. For some reason he felt the box was there. However, there is still the appraiser's missing notes. Perhaps . . . ."

Dropping this thought, the sleuth went to another one.

"Let me present a situation. The appraiser fin-
ishes his work. Someone returns the Manheim file
to its appointed place. Where would that be?"

"I don't know," was Frisbee's prompt reply.
"That is also a closely guarded secret. You realize of
course . . ." Frisbee checked himself. "No, perhaps
you don't. Leicester Ltd. has always been a one man
operation. The staff is not involved in decisions. He
doesn't have a board of directors, lucky fellow. In
times gone by, some of his best moves in or out of
situations were made very quickly and it was necessary for him to have documents, papers, whatever
was involved, at hand."

"Then the investment house is, in effect, a bank
with all of the valuables entrusted to it on the
premises."

"Correct, Holmes. I know about Leicester's file
arrangement but don't have the foggiest as to where
they are hidden."

"Would his account executives know?"

Frisbee shrugged. "The old man can't be there all
the time. I would guess all three of them know simply because of the mechanics of the matter. The
secretaries or bookkeeper surely don't. Nor the receptionist. Don't quote me on this gentlemen, but
the security arrangements at Leicester Ltd. are
equal to those of Inter-Ocean. Leicester owns the
building; the place is a fortress."

I was deeply grateful that the matter of a fee had
been dealt with. Call anything impregnable and all
of Holmes' instincts demanded that he prove other-

wise with no thought of recompense.

"I'm going to have a lot of questions for Frontnoy Leicester that I don't think he will want to answer." The sleuth sounded resigned.

"He's not too accessible either," stated Frisbee. "Would you like me to make some moves regarding your meeting with him?"

"Let's wait," said Holmes. "At the moment I'm not anxious to have you identified as my client. You don't, by chance, have an account with him?"

Frisbee shuddered. "Any investments of mine would have to be through Inter-Ocean. If it was breathed otherwise, it might start a run on the bank."

"Of course," replied Holmes, annoyed with himself for overlooking this.

"I know someone who deals through him," I said, delighted to make a contribution to the discussion.

"Do you now, Watson?"

"Lady Teasdale. Patient of mine. You attended one of her teas."

Now it was Holmes who shuddered. "We'll certainly bear that fact in mind, old fellow. Could well be useful."

"Chronic insomnia," I informed Frisbee. "Brought on by overindulgence, but that's classified information."

The banker understood.

"By the by," said the sleuth, "do you know the brand of cigarettes that Wyndhaven used?"

Frisbee's response was swift.

"He never smoked in his life."

There was a pregnant pause, broken by the sleuth.

"You asked yourself what you could tell us that could be of help," he said to the banker. "Believe me, you've helped."

6

The Commissioner and the Financier

When we departed from Simpsons, Phineas Portney—cabby extraordinaire—was awaiting us with news as well as his vehicle.

"Jones from the Yard was here, Mr. Holmes. Wanted my version of the fracas we 'ad. Precious little I could tell him 'cept that them two constables what showed up were eyewitnesses to the whole blame thing."

"I did wonder about their opportune arrival." Holmes shot a suspicious glance at me but did not pursue the matter. "You told Jones where we were?" he continued, indicating the restaurant.

"Yes sir, but 'e didn't want to intrude. Said he'd be waiting fer you at Baker Street."

"Accommodating. We shall not disappoint him."

Our peaceful return to 221B was a far cry from our departure. It crossed my mind that Holmes must have Portney, like others, on his payroll. I kept a loose set of books on our finances, and there was an alarming amount allocated to "research." Since Holmes' research principally consisted of daily journals, the files and case books, plus his encyclopedic memory, it took no genius to figure where that money went. However, the sleuth always gave the red-nosed Phineas a generous tip. To keep him from gravitating to cheaper brands was Holmes' explanation.

We found Athelney Jones pacing the hall outside our door, looking contrite and nervous at the same time.

"Mr. Holmes . . ." he began, but the sleuth cut him off.

"Have you identified our recent assailants?" he asked as we entered our chambers.

"Yes, Sir. Former members of Whitey Burke's London Duster gang. Word is they split with Whitey and are on their own."

"Did they peach about who put them up to the job?"

"No, Sir, and I don't think they will. With two of our boys as witnesses, they know they've had it and there's not a chance of a lessening of charges or sentences. Mr. Holmes. . . . "

"It was too well planned," stated the sleuth. "I suspect another professional in the wings. The carriage overtaking us was fairly standard, but the rifle in the window of the house as a back-up is another thing."

"Mr. Holmes . . ." began Jones again, with a forlorn air.

"Could have been the brainchild of Negretto Sylvius, but we'll let that go for the moment. Well, what is it Jones?"

"I'm due at the Commissioner's office in forty minutes." There was a naked plea in the inspector's voice and manner.

"Jones, Jones, what am I to do with you? I told you what to say to Brickstone last evening."

"I did, Mr. Holmes, word for word."

"What is the name of your friend on the Beacon?"

"Blatt, Sir. . . ."

"Well, you promptly blatted everything to him, also word for word."

"It was in confidence, Mr. Holmes."

"In confidence? To a reporter?" Holmes looked heavenward and then collected himself. "All right. Tell the Commissioner that you still suspect foul play in the Wyndhaven matter. Then tell him about the street battle. He already knows but tell him anyway. Say you suspect a connection between the two matters. But tell that only to the Commissioner. Don't breathe a word to anyone else. If I am any judge, this web will take a while to untangle, and we want no public hue and cry. In fact, the less said about the attack on Watson and myself, the better."

"I won't breathe a word, not even to my wife Sophie. Not even to my dog Rosenkavalier."

From Holmes' expression, I judged that he harbored a sudden suspicion relative to his hearing.

"Jones," he said slowly, "you did say that you had a dog named Rosenkavalier?"

"Fine animal, Mr. Holmes."

"I'm sure."

"I was given two 'fer free' to the opera, and Sophie and me. . . ."

"Never mind," interrupted the sleuth. "I get the idea. Though naught will come of it, you are going to check the names of Leicester's staff with the records at the Yard, are you not?"

"Right on, Mr. Holmes. I hadn't gotten 'round to that."

"But you will, so don't let us detain you from your diligent pursuit of duty."

"I'm off, Mr. Holmes," said Athelney Jones, and he was.

My friend regarded me with twinkling eyes. "Did I overplay the role of the stern schoolmaster, Watson?"

I was shaking my head. "If anyone suspected your pawkish sense of humor . . . but no mind. Jones is unusual to say the least."

I secured my stethoscope from its hook on the back of our hall door and coiled it in the crown of my topper.

"Knowing you, Holmes, it is time for meditation. I'll devote the afternoon to some overdue patient calls."

"You might drop in on Lady Teasdale," suggested the sleuth. "She will have read about Wyndhaven and by now it has probably leaked that he died at Leicester Ltd. She might have some comments to make about that establishment."

"Should have thought of that myself. By the by, any ideas on what the Commissioner has in mind?"

"Brickstone is but recent to his post, and I have not gotten to really know the man. There may be some surprises in store for us tomorrow morning."

Holmes hit the mark dead center, as I learned when we were ushered into the office of Cecil Brickstone the following day.

The commissioner dismissed his assistant, got us seated, offered cigars and broached what was on his mind with commendable speed.

"Look here, Holmes, things would be simpler if young Hopkins had less imagination and you hadn't gotten involved in this. Referring to Wyndhaven, of course. The autopsy indicates nothing but a failure of the heart. Now I want to reassure myself. You have good cause to think he was murdered, correct?"

"Yes, Commissioner. For one thing, his notes. . . ."

"No mind, no mind, your saying it is enough. That attempt on you and Watson here rather bears it out."

"I'm in hopes we can play that incident down," said Holmes. "You see. . . ."

"I've already done what I could about that. A soft key approach. Now I want to make one thing clear."

The commissioner paused as though to marshal the full force of his message, and alarm bells rang in my mind. "Here we go," I thought. "If this fellow takes a stern stand, he'll have something of a tartar on his hands with Holmes."

"Notoriety and newspaper stories are something that a man like Frontnoy Leicester avoids at all cost. Unless they are carefully programmed interviews about his triumphs, of course. We'll never keep the lid on where that appraiser chap died, for it's out now and we'd best accept the fact. Leicester has the necessary connections to apply pressure, to try to get this thing out of the way and under the rug. The first message from, shall we say, an influential source has already arrived. More will follow. How you are going to prove that a man who died of a heart stoppage was murdered evades me, but you will . . . you will."

Now it was I who was in some doubt as to what I had just heard, but it seemed that further surprises were in order.

"You go ahead in your own way and resolve this matter. My office can withstand any attempts at a solution of expediency."

I rather think Holmes was more amazed than I at this turn of events.

"That's very considerate of you, Commissioner," he began, but got no further.

"Good heavens man, as much as I would enjoy a reputation for fearless integrity, we must accept the motive of self-preservation. Do you think I want the P.M., Bellinger, on my neck or the irascible Lord

Cantlemere?* Worse yet, if I had a hand at tangling up the investigation of the world's greatest criminologist, it is not hard to picture a summons to Windsor from a certain august lady. But I would not return with a splendid emerald tie pin.** No no. Instead, I would be in search of a post. Holmes, what position would you say is suitable for an ex-commissioner of police?"

"Retirement."

Brickstone slapped his knee approvingly. "Exactly what I have in mind after long and meritorious service. To achieve that. . . ."

He rose from his desk and crossed to the nearest window, indicating the outside scene.

". . .I have that to contend with. A mushrooming London. Even back in '78 the official population figure was three-and-a-half million and everyone knew it was a million short. There are a hundred thousand paupers out there and fifteen hundred who sleep on benches on the Embankment or in Trafalgar Square, two hundred and ninety pawnbrokers, and enough prostitutes to equal in number the army of some European countries. We've got our soldier boys spread over the globe and our ships on

---

*It is presumed that this was the illustrious Lord Bellinger's third term as Prime Minister of Britain, since it must follow "The Adventure of the Mazarin Stone." Prior to the theft of the great crown diamond, the influential Lord Cantlemere was a stern critic of Holmes, but when the sleuth recovered the Mazarin Stone, he became one of Holmes' most dedicated supporters.

**Commissioner Brickstone was referring to Sherlock Holmes' rewarding experience following his solution of the matter involving the Bruce-Partington Plans.

every sea, but it's not worth a button if we can't hold the reins here at home. We've got good men because they came up through the ranks. I don't mean the likes of Jones. Man's an imbecile, but he has his uses. Chap hasn't gotten in your way, has he?"

"No, Commissioner. I think I can say that he is trying his best."

"That's something. Not much, but something. No, I mean chaps like MacDonald, Gregson, possibly young Hopkins, who shows promise, and their ilk. But we've got to have help and I'm counting on Mr. Sherlock Holmes and you, Watson, good fellow."

Brickstone returned to his desk with a sigh.

"That's it. We've got ourselves lined up, I hope. I've arranged a meeting with Frontnoy Leicester for you at noon if that's agreeable."

Holmes nodded.

"Splendid. Good hunting and all that."

During our departure from the commissioner's office, and for some moments thereafter, I can truthfully say that Holmes could not come up with one word. Nor could I.

When we were ushered into the private office of Frontnoy Leicester, I anticipated that Holmes would be questioning a resentful man and would have sticky going. I should have known better, simply because this entire case had been a series of surprises to this point.

"Mr. Holmes. Dr. Watson. Do be seated." Leicester's voice and manner were ebullient and there was that touch of the entrepreneur, that effort to put one at ease and, therefore, more susceptible to suggestion.

"Made a frightful blunder in connection with you chaps," continued the financial wizard."Let drop to my wife that Brickstone wanted us to touch wickets. It was all I could do to dissuade the dear woman from coming to the office on some pretext just to get a glimpse of the famous Sherlock Holmes. As you may gather, Dr. Watson, she's read every one of your stories; more than once I suspect."

I mumbled something as befits a humble author, but I doubt if Leicester heard me, for he segued quickly into the purpose of our visit.

"Let's have at it, shall we, regarding the unfortunate Wyndhaven? Knew him for years, you know. Just wish the dear fellow had picked a different spot to say goodbye to the world."

By now the whole force of his personality was directed at Holmes.

"Am told you are dead set that there's more to it than heart failure. Could you tell me why, Mr. Holmes?"

"I could," replied the sleuth, "but then you might let it slip to your good wife and ruin the suspense of one of Watson's stories for her."

Leicester chuckled and shook his head, but underneath his manner sobered as though he were facing more than he wished to.

"That's the deftest refusal I can remember, Sir. Obviously I can't divert you from your pattern of doing things. Why should I expect to?"

Leicester shrugged as though in surrender, but the shrewd and canny look in his keen eyes did not desert him.

"Where, then, shall we start?"

"I'm most interested in the last time you saw the deceased," said Holmes.

"Reasonable, and the same question that would pique me, were I a consulting detective which, praise be, I'm not. However, I may prove to be one of the best witnesses you've had, for nature blessed me with a photographic memory. If I can recreate the picture in my mind, where people stood and all that, I can give you the chain of events just as they happened."

The old man leaned back in his large desk chair and, as his eyes closed, his face tilted upwards. I did not know if this was some sham of his or not, but it was certainly unusual.

"It was mid-afternoon and I was returning here after a meeting with some very knowledgeable gentlemen who shall remain nameless."

I noted the muscles in his scrawny neck tighten as though he was not to be dissuaded on this point.

"A line of action in the market came to me in my carriage, and I made a decision coming up in the lift. As a consequence, I was in search of the first available pair of legs when I arrived in the reception room, and there was Weems just coming from the visitor's office."

Holmes threw a quick look in my direction, and I knew he had identified the visitor's office as the small room not far from the receptionist's desk where Wyndhaven's body was found. A place for clients to retreat if in need of making notes, considering their position, or whatever else might come to their minds. Another of those touches in an establishment devoted to customer needs, or whims for that matter.

"I asked Weems if Wyndhaven had shown up, and he indicated that he had, gesturing towards the visitor's office, which was as far as I allowed him to get. I took him by the arm and walked him away from the receptionist's desk, for my orders were private, you see.

" 'I'll take care of Wyndhaven,' I said. 'Get your coat and hustle over to the Grain Pit. You just might make it before the closing bell. Locate Reicher and give him an order for my account. Three months' option, 10,000 bushels of Alamargado wheat at the opening market.' Weems started to say something, about the Manheim File no doubt, but I cut him short. 'Move man! There's little time. Phone me on my private line whether you make it or not. Then take what's left of the day off.' I didn't wait to see what he did, for my boys jump when I talk like that. I went right to the visitor's office and Wyndhaven."

The old man's eyes opened and he lowered his chin to regard us both.

"Have we got it so far?"

Since Holmes did not come up with an immediate question, that curiosity which has plagued me throughout my life took control.

"Mr. Leicester, what is the Grain Pit and, while we're at it, what was the meaning of your order?"

Rather than registering boredom at my ignorance of such matters, Leicester appeared delighted.

"Bless you Doctor, for I hoped someone would ask. I have to do a lot of explaining to clients on occasion and delight in keeping my hand in. The Pit is but a name for the place where commodity futures are handled. Ours here in London doesn't match the one in Chicago by any means, but we generate a bit of action. Reicher is the man I deal with there. As for my order, I wanted an option . . . a right . . . for three months to buy 10,000 bushels of wheat at the price quoted at the opening of business the next morning."

"What would you ever do with all that wheat?"

"I shall never even see it, Doctor. For that matter, the man that sells me the option probably doesn't even own it."

My head was shaking in a most discouraged manner, which delighted Leicester even more. Through my mind flashed a thought voiced by Holmes some time back. "The expert invariably welcomes the opportunity of proving why he is an expert."

"We're dealing in futures, Doctor. If the price of wheat goes up, and I think it will, I have the right to buy it under the market. Therefore, my option becomes valuable and I can sell it at a profit."

"Suppose the price goes down?"

"Then I am out my option money, a pittance compared with the price of the wheat."

"Could you not have reached this Reicher by phone?" asked Holmes.

"If you gentlemen ever wish to really understand the meaning of pandemonium, I suggest you visit the Pit. My contact there is on the floor taking orders, arranging buys and sells constantly. Little chance of reaching him by phone."

"Could you not have called him after the close of business?" suggested Holmes quietly.

"You are beginning to see through me, Mr. Holmes. You're right, of course, but I had a scheme. I wanted Weems at the Pit if he could arrive before closing."

"Why was that important?" I blurted out.

"Had he gotten there on time, he would have been seen placing an order. He is known as one of my men, and somebody would have been interested— and the order would have leaked. Commodities are highly susceptible to suggestion. I would have called Reicher at his home and cancelled my order, anticipating a rise in option prices come morning. Monkey see, monkey do. Then when they sagged back, option prices I mean, I would have stepped in. As it was, Weems didn't make it and he phoned me in my office to tell me so. I reached Reicher via phone that evening and gave him my order then. The idea of Weems was just an effort to get what I wanted at a lower price. It's all a gamble you know, but big profits don't come to those who run scared."

"Or those with pedestrian, rather than innovative methods," said Holmes, and there was a gleam of admiration in his eyes.

"Bless me," exclaimed Leicester, "this could be the beginning of a long friendship. But you wish to know more about Wyndhaven. I exchanged greetings with him. We had been through this before. Then I got him the Manheim File. I had several calls to make and wanted my private line free when Weems checked back, so I told Wyndhaven to call me when he was finished. After Weems came through with the news that he had not gotten to the Grain Pit on time, things were quiet, so I dismissed the rest of the staff. Then some matter came up that I hadn't anticipated, and I was busy till closing time. Wyndhaven was still at it, so I told him when he finished to place the file on this desk here."

Leicester thumped his desk for emphasis.

"I instructed him to then activate the spring lock on my door and take his leave. When the door to this office is spring-locked, no one can open it save me. The file was safe in here, and I certainly had no doubts about Wyndhaven. Knew the man for a quarter of a century, you see."

"So you had no worries about the Manheim File when Inspector Hopkins called you," said Holmes.

"Not when he checked my office door and assured me it was locked."

"Suppose the appraiser had finished before your departure? Where would the file have been put?"

"Where it came from. An artful question, Mr. Holmes, but that's all the answer I'm giving. You might attempt to learn through official channels, but I assure you it would result in a legal battle."

"What about the file itself?"

"Viewing its contents would also necessitate a court battle."

"We could make a trade," suggested Holmes. I sensed he was enjoying himself. "I'll tell you how I know Wyndhaven was murdered and you let me view, with an associate, the Manheim securities. What say?"

Leicester's response was swift. "I fear we will both have to curb our curiosity, Mr. Holmes."

At this point, my previous reference to reaching an impasse would have been appropriate.

7

The Plan

As we left the investment firm, Holmes drew my attention to the ground floor arrangement of the office building. The main lobby housed the lifts which serviced the first seven stories. The one which we had used was situated in a different and smaller area, not connected to the lobby at all. With other things to think of, this division had not impressed itself on my mind before.

"Holmes, it is obviously wasteful of space. Why this separation, do you suppose?"

"The private lift, Watson, is the only one that goes to the eighth floor. No way stations between the ground floor and the Leicester office either. The stairwell, necessary because of the building codes, does not connect with the other floors either. Leicester's place of business can only be reached through this entry way we are now in. It is completely cut off from the rest of the building."

"A fine arrangement for Leicester. With a watchman down here, it's nigh onto impossible to reach his offices unless announced and passed through.

Surely the financier did not redesign the ground
floor in this manner after purchasing the building
from the Savage interests?"

"No, the top floor was designed by the architect as
his living quarters. Savage was at the pinnacle of his
profession and is still considered in the same breath
with Shaw and Francis Fowler. His buildings are
beautiful in shape and form, and he was inordinate-
ly fond of members of the opposite sex boasting the
same attributes. Savage arranged things so that it
was impossible for him to be surprised by an indignant husband with mayhem in mind."

Holmes hailed a hansom, for Portney was not on
duty. He directed the driver towards The Strand.

"What now?" I asked.

"Waldo Wynn-Chichester's bookstore. I recall a
literary review of *His Final Creation*, subtitled 'The
Story of the Savage Building.' The book is well
thought of by architects and engineers. Possibly
Wynn-Chichester has a copy."

"What is he up to now?" I thought. "Suddenly
the Savage Building has become important to him."

I always enjoyed visiting Wynn-Chichester's
place of business since he made a practice of keeping
a good stock of my books. There had been indications that he read them as well. Just off The Strand,
Wynn-Chichester's was the place to locate something of a specialized nature, that being his major
source of sales. The owner knew of the book Holmes
wanted and, after rummaging around a bit, was able
to locate a copy. The sleuth stood by a window in the

wintery light and leafed through it with special attention to a number of fold-out pages which, I ascertained, were reproductions of blueprints.

"That's it," I thought. "He has an idea and wants to go over the original blueprints of the Savage Building." This had all the earmarks of one of those breaking and entering operations, which the unofficial Holmes was not averse to at all.

Whenever I tried to mimic my friend in the field of inference and drew a conclusion from the facts at hand, I was conditioned to a surprise, with developments not as I had imagined them at all. The surprise in this case was that I was on the right track.

First off, upon our return to Baker Street, Holmes had Billy on the go with messages. Then he settled down with the Savage book, giving it a "two pipe" study and making numeric notations at the desk. I tried to busy myself with the odds and ends that accumulate in a day's living, but abandoned this to sum up, in my mind, my own views regarding the Wyndhaven affair. I wished to be ready if there was a discussion of the matter, a possibility at this stage.

Holmes balled up the paper on which he had been making notes and threw it into the wastebasket. Closing the book, *His Final Creation*, and shoving it to a corner of our desk's surface, he turned to me.

"Old chap, we'd best stop wandering around getting people's versions of the appraiser's end and take some action of our own."

"Surely you haven't solved the matter?"

"I know very little indeed save that, for several

reasons, I'm sure that Wyndhaven's death was contrived. Haven't the foggiest as to the culprit or, for
that matter, the motive which might well lead to the
villain of the piece."

"You do feel the reason involves the Manheim File?"

"My apologies. That's true. Manheim's portfolio
seems our best lead and we've got to follow up on it.
Frontnoy Leicester was cooperation personified till
we got to that matter. Of course, we could go to
Berlin and ask the steel tycoon. I believe he would
give us a hand, but just the listing of his security
holdings and whatever else he has with Leicester
might not turn the trick. Then there is the matter of
time. Commissioner Brickstone has given us some
latitude in that respect, but there are going to be
questions. That reporter, Blatt, has found something to keep his by-line prominently displayed.
Why isn't simple heart failure called just that? Why
the delay in the official listing of the matter? Athelney Jones' report and my opinion are all that stands
in the way of the whole thing being dropped."

"Jones' report and your opinion are the same
thing, are they not?"

"Touché again, Watson. I find myself saying that
more and more with you. Perhaps I shall retire to
bee-keeping on the Sussex Downs sooner than
anticipated."

"Come now, Holmes, be serious. You've got me
on tenterhooks, for it's not often you go over a case."

The sleuth's bantering air disappeared and his
sharp features softened momentarily.

"Ever patient, Watson—my only true confidant. All right, revelations though they be limited. I know how the man was killed but not the manner of the doing."

It was my turn to gaze upward for divine intervention.

"Holmes, that statement only serves to increase my confusion. You must realize that."

"True." My friend sighed. "Permit me to bypass that piece of the puzzle, for I wish to think more on it myself. The motive eludes us, but I propose to take action on that. As to the suspects, it would seem that they are limited to members of the Leicester organization."

"Or the old fellow himself," I suggested.

"A possibility. Far-fetched, perhaps, but not to be overlooked. Now we come to a formidable impasse. Leicester says he dismissed his staff prior to his own departure. Since we can and will check this when questioning his people, I hardly think he could be misleading us. Question: Only Wyndhaven remained in the offices and someone returned to deal with him; how was that accomplished?"

"The watchman," I exclaimed. "He would certainly have told Hopkins or Jones if one of the group had returned."

"That individual merits our attention, of course. You will admit that the layout of the building seems to give our suspects an alibi; all of them."

"Leaving only the watchman and the porter."

"The possibility of one or both of them as suspects

did cross my mind, but fleetingly. I cannot imagine either of them having a motive."

What seemed like an inspiration forced itself upon me.

"Holmes, suppose Wyndhaven was dead before Leicester departed from the premises?"

Holmes' eyes lit up with either approval or gratitude, I knew not which.

"Our years together have not been wasted. Bravo, old chap. I was wondering if that would occur to you."

"We have but his word that he instructed Wyndhaven regarding the Manheim File and then departed. As you pointed out to Hopkins, his leaving a non-employee alone in the offices did sound a bit thin."

"What is your conclusion?"

"It would seem I have no choice. As of now, old man Leicester is the prime suspect."

"I agree," replied Holmes, causing my chest to swell with pride. "As with our watchman and porter, the motive is hard to envision. Recall, he stated relative to Wyndhaven, 'we had been through this before.' Ergo, the appraiser had gone over someone's assets previously. Why would this particular inspection drive Leicester to murder? His financial stability is legendary."

"Again, Holmes, we only have his word as to that."

"I believe you are rather intrigued with the financier as the culprit."

"He seems the only one with opportunity," I replied, somewhat defensively.

In a dry tone, Holmes gave me further food for thought.

"Also, the only suspect we have interviewed."

Had I been able to summon a rebuttal to this, it would have remained unsaid, for we had visitors. First Wallingford and, on his heels, came the redoubtable Slim Gilligan. Ah ha, I thought, the results of the messages that Holmes had dispatched Billy with.

As readers of previous adventures of Sherlock Holmes well know, Gilligan had been the finest cracksman of our time prior to casting his lot with the great detective. It was Holmes who had gotten the goods on Slim following what proved to be his last escapade outside the law. After paying his debt to society, Gilligan had philosophically accepted the fact that opening burglar-proof safes, making unbelievable entries and exits and eluding Sherlock Holmes at the same time was just too much for one man. So he became a vital cog in the mechanism that my friend had put together and the sleuth's major pipeline to the land of the lawless. A whisper on a dark street, a rumor that something was "coming down" in a haunt of the ungodly, and the odds were good that Gilligan would hear it. A modus operandi not on file in that vast storehouse of Holmes' mind might well spark recognition in the cracksman's.

Holmes, in jest, called "Get Rich Quick" Wallingford his gift from our American cousins. So deft

had the former confidence man been that there were
no extradition proceedings when he decided that the
climate was warmish in his homeland and a trans-
oceanic trip was called for. When this handsome and
ingratiating fellow was brought into contact with
Holmes, his way of living underwent a change,
which he stated was more exciting and more peaceful at the same time. He had once told me, "I prefer
looking Holmes in the eye rather than looking over
my shoulder in fear of finding him there."

So, I thought to myself, Holmes has a group effort
planned and has called in members of what his
brother, Mycroft, referred to as "that rag-tag army
that follows your flag, Sherlock."

They were not rag-tag, as Mycroft Holmes well
knew, and I might not be writing these words but for
Gilligan's rescue effort during a fracas at the Non-
pareil Club. That, however, is another story.

Automatically, I sent Billy for some cold stout
from below whilst I busied myself at the spirit cabinet with a gin concoction, unknown in the British
Isles. Wallingford had given me the formula.

"I was wondering if we'd see some action," said
the American. "The press coverage has been
considerable."

"The interest of the daily journals proved beneficial in one respect," said Holmes. "It stimulated
certain unknowns into taking action when they
might otherwise have lain low. Unfortunately, their
action seems directed at Watson and myself."

"I heard about that, Gov." There was an ugly

look about Gilligan. "You and the Doc sure took care of Burke's boys, though it's said that bunch split with Whitey."

"So we heard and I had nothing to do with what happened to them." Knowing that Gilligan considered an attack on either or both of us as a personal affront, Holmes pressed on.

"Are you familiar with the Savage Building, Slim?"

"I knows where it is."

"It's a beauty. Tight as a drum but we've got some business there. Nighttime business."

"I knew it," I thought to myself. "Holmes has a reason for whatever he's planning, but he's working it so that he'll prove the supposedly invulnerable offices of Leicester Ltd. are not inaccessible after all." Then I had a second thought. "He could be thinking of the suspects other than Leicester himself. If Holmes and Slim can figure out a way to get into the suite of offices undetected, someone else might have used the same means."

"You want I should case this building, Gov?" Gilligan's eyes were glistening. "I figure it's the Leicester office you're interested in."

"After we've gone over an idea, Slim, you check it out as best you can. Here's the situation. There's a private entrance with watchman to the only lift that goes up to the eighth floor where the office is. The street door is formidable, for I took a good look at it. The lift has a safety hatch."

Gilligan was nodding. "It would have to, to comply with the building commission's safety code."

"A moment," I said, trying to follow this conversation. "I was in that lift with you, Holmes. What is this hatch you refer to?"

"Quite similar to the one in our carriage that you popped through when we were set upon, Watson. Every public lift has to have a trap in the ceiling. If there is a mechanical failure, it enables occupants to reach the roof. It also facilitates matters for a work crew checking the cables or making repairs."

"I didn't see it."

"You didn't look upwards, old chap. Few people do in a lift."

"This trap or hatch is your key to getting in?" asked Wallingford.

"In part. When we get to the eighth floor, there's a portfolio of securities that we're going to check out. That's where you come in Wally."

"What am I looking for?"

"I don't really know. Whatever someone wants kept secret. Wants it enough to commit murder."

"Do my best," stated the former confidence man.

"Gov," said Gilligan tentatively, "there's somethin' bothers me a mite. You said one door from the street." Holmes nodded. "Then there's one lift and one watchman. Now that fellow hasn't got much to keep his eye on. How do we get around him?"

"By doing just that," replied Holmes. "We're going around him. During the day we're going to get you through that trap and onto the top of the lift.

Not the most comfortable place to spend some time, but it can't be helped."

"Comes with the job, Gov," stated the philosophical Gilligan.

"Darkness falls and the office is empty," continued Holmes. "You get back into the lift and run it to the basement. That is another tough proposition, and we couldn't get in from the outside, for I checked it carefully. But with you on the inside, Slim, it's a different story."

My mind was racing. "When did he do all this?" I thought to myself. Then I recalled that afternoon when I made patient calls. I had thought my friend was reviewing things in his mind, but he must have gone out, in one of his innumerable disguises, no doubt.

"Isn't everyone who enters checked by the watchman?" I exclaimed. "How do we get Slim into the lift?"

"That, Watson, is where you come in."

"Me? I thought I was but the audience to this scheme."

"Old chap, you are vital to the operation."

Of course, I always wanted to take an active part in one of Holmes' investigations, especially since that Lady Carfax matter, which I had bungled so badly. However, my heart sank at my friend's words, but then I rallied with the thought that I had met with some success in "The Sacred Sword" matter.

"Please, Holmes, would you go over my part slowly. Slim and Wallingford here have experience in such matters. They grasp your words readily, but

I am not that proficient."

The sleuth reverted to his familiar device of the Socratical answer.

"You did visit Lady Teasdale when making your rounds, I trust?"

"Yes, but she made no mention of the newspaper story or the Leicester organization, and I did not feel it wise to prompt her."

"Good thinking, Watson."

"Lady Teasdale?" Wallingford was intrigued. "The widow of the shipping magnate?"

"Do you know her?" asked Holmes quickly.

"No, but in my work . . . former work . . . rich widows were an interesting subject."

"She is a patient of mine," I said in, I hope, an offhanded manner. I didn't add that she was one of few—small wonder, with all the running around I did with Holmes.

"Lady Teasdale is also a client of Leicester Ltd.," stated Holmes.

Wallingford's lips pursed in a soundless whistle. "Good show, Doctor, and very convenient."

Holmes' brow was furrowed. "Do you think, Watson, that you can persuade her ladyship to accept a part, as 'twere, in our little playlet?"

Suddenly, midst all this expert plotting and planning, I was the central figure, an unusual occurrence indeed.

"I think Lady Teasdale's major problem is boredom. I'll wager the prospect of being involved in an investigation of Sherlock Holmes' will prove irresistible."

8
The Inside Man

I made a brave show and spoke with conviction when it was but a matter of words. However, I suffered many a worrysome moment when the action portion of convincing her ladyship was upon me.

Seeing her was no problem and explaining away the presence of Wallingford was equally simple. Then I had to get down to it, trying to exhibit confidence and treating the whole idea as something of a lark. Her ladyship was completely surprised, considerably thrilled, and then began to express doubts as to her ability to carry it off. I noted, however, that she was very glad to receive my assurances, and there was a verve and excited expectation about her that I had not been able to produce as her doctor. When I finally got a tentative agreement, it was time for the shock troops, and I brought Wallingford into the discussion. No one could "set the scene" or gently rehearse her ladyship better than he. Since she was but playing herself in this proposed vignette, there were not too many problems to cope with, and Wallingford led her through the planned actions so cleverly that she did not even realize she was being coached. But then, my American friend had set up so many "marks" in his time that it was old hat to him.

So it was that four of us entered the hallway of the Savage Building leading to the private lift on the afternoon of the following day. The prospect of an operation without the presence of Holmes filled me with dread, but Wallingford had given me a bit of coaching as well. Her ladyship was undoubtedly nervous, which made her more haughty and regal than ever; not a bad thing at all.

The watchman, appointment list in hand, who barred our passage, was suitably impressed; nay, somewhat awed.

"Lady Teasdale and party," entoned my patient. "I'm expected, naturally."

As he consulted his list (from habit), her ladyship indicated her retinue. "My personal physician, Dr. Watson." When the watchman nodded in recognition, for he had seen me before, Lady Teasdale waved bejeweled fingers at Wallingford and Gilligan. "My secretary and driver."

As her ladyship's temporary driver, Gilligan seemed only slightly uncomfortable in livery.

I suspected that Wallingford must feel proud over the performance of her ladyship. Her grand manner had the desired effect. After making a check opposite the appointment time listed, the watchman led us towards the lift in quite a subsubservient manner.

As he was about to usher us inside, Lady Teasdale gasped and managed to look quite ill.

"Doctor . . . Doctor, it's the vapors," she mumbled, staggering against the watchman. He was forced to support her as she began to swoon, calling to Gilligan as she did so.

"My salts, Billings, in the carriage. Quickly."

Wallingford and I positioned ourselves as planned, while we assisted the watchman in maneuvering a seemingly semi-conscious woman to the customary bench opposite the lift. Effectively screened, Gilligan slipped into the lift instead of racing for the fictional salts as ordered. There was much fanning interspersed with moans from her ladyship before she recovered sufficiently to allow me to assist her into our objective. Wallingford had an aside for the watchman, delivered in a confidential tone.

"Happens all the time. She will be quite all right and forget about it in a moment."

"Where's the driver fellow?" he asked.

"Getting ready for a snooze in the carriage," replied Wallingford with a knowing wink. "He's been with her ladyship for a long time. If he does come back, you can send him up, but I wouldn't wager on it."

With the man's suspicions allayed, Wallingford joined us. The agile Gilligan had disappeared and the trap was back in place. Slim was the unknown passenger on the roof as we rode upwards to the eighth floor.

Wallingford and I seated ourselves in the reception area as Lady Teasdale was ushered into the

visitor's office by her account executive who happened to be Macy. Possibly, as her ladyship went
through pre-determined questions relative to her
holdings, the attentive Mr. Macy was surprised at
the absence of his client's usual petulance or by the
speed with which Lady Teasdale assured herself of
her solvency. More likely, he was just grateful as he
saw us to the lift, which returned us to the ground
floor. The watchman was as attentive as the account
executive and trusted that her ladyship had completely recovered. He was airily informed that she
had, as my dear patient, anticipated the end of this
frightening and quite beguiling adventure, surely
with regrets. I'm certain she had enjoyed her unusual debut in the performing arts and Wallingford was
quite at home, naturally. Only I felt immense relief
as we escaped to the outside world.

No matter! It was over and our job was done. The
"inside man" was planted.

I may recoil from suiting actions to words, but the
waiting is definitely the worst part of an investigation. Though Holmes drove himself and railed
against ineptitude, being most caustic as regards
himself, he did have the ability to turn off. When
naught was to be gained by action, and one had but
to allow for the passage of time, he unwound, refuel-
ing his store of energies. Though I reasoned that this
was the only sensible course, I found it hard to
follow.

After our play-acting adventure, Wallingford and
I were busy doing the right thing by Lady Teasdale.

En route to her residence, we made much of her contribution, and that was not fabrication. She was the only client of the investment house that I knew of. Holmes might have been able to unearth another, but he might not.

The dear, though sometimes aggravating, woman insisted that we join her in a victory cup. This turned out to be a pleasant interlude with chilled, hollow-stemmed champagne glasses that boasted an excellent vintage. The late Basil Teasdale's cellar had a reputation for excellence which I can attest to. Lady Teasdale, quite flushed from the "bubbly" and the culmination of an occurrence unique for a lady of fashion, was batting her eyelashes furiously at Wallingford as we made our escape with repeated promises that she would be the first to know the end result of this baffling case. Inasmuch as we had been vague about the matter, I doubted that the culmination, when it came, would make much sense to her. I also suspected that the handsome Wallingford was her principal interest. Both of these assumptions proved incorrect.

I urged the driver of the hansom we hailed to return us to Baker Street at his best speed. I rather pictured Holmes, whose trademark was a glacial calm when involved in a matter, as pacing our floor with anxiety regarding a plan executed without benefit of his sure hand. If so, he concealed any trepidations upon our arrival, an easy task considering Wallingford's opening words.

"Like the cat's whiskers. Nothing to it."

9
Nighttime Excursion

It was now that the onerous waiting began, for we could make no move until the close of the day's business and the departure of those concerned from the office building. A feeling of restlessness and a desire to get a move on plagued me till the thought of Gilligan cooled my impatience. There he was in the dark and dust of the shaft, riding up and down and having to be deuced careful about movement or sound when there were passengers below him.

A move prior to the hour of seven would have been rash indeed, so that was our standby hour. Under the cover of night, Holmes, Wallingford and I filtered singly and silently into the rear area of the Savage Building where we congregated at the ramp leading down to the freight entrance. It had been agreed that this was our only chance. The windows were protected by metal bars set deep in masonry and would have required a blowtorch or a bull chain with an elephant at one end.

The minutes ticked by as I shifted my weight from one foot to the other. The night wind was cold and I kept my muffler and topcoat close about me. There seemed little chance of our presence being revealed. The streets of the financial district, teeming with hurrying people by day, resembled an abandoned city at night. It was as though a great, celestial broom had swept away all life. With no residences in the area, no light shown from windows and not a pedestrian or a carriage was to be seen. But I knew that behind those dark windows and marble façades was the unseen army—the watchmèn and security personnel that guarded the wealth of London.

In the heart of the great city, the silence of this section sensitized our hearing, and we turned as one when there was a faint scratching followed by an authoritative click. The origin of this welcome break in the monotony of our vigil was the great lock on the freight door. Slowly the pattern of deep shadows close to the building, cast by a fitful moon, altered and I realized that the door was now ajar.

Holmes was at the aperture in a trice.

"Slim?" he whispered.

"Right on, Gov," was the welcome response. In Holmes' wake, we slipped inside and closed the metal door. Before the faint light from outside was cut off, I saw Holmes pass the cracksman his burglar kit, which we had brought with us. The sophisticated tools within were, for the most part, one-of-a-kind Gilligan creations. There was also a small bulls-eye lantern, which the cracksman used sparingly as he guided us to the lift that had been his roost for some hours.

"All clear upstairs, Gov."

"Did anything of interest occur to reward your patience?" inquired Holmes.

"Can't say that it did. I 'ad it brought home to me that life 'as its ups and downs."

As we entered the lift, an alarming thought struck me.

"Holmes! Gilligan! Does this thing have a floor indicator? The watchman might note its moving."

"Good show, Watson. A cautious thought," said Holmes approvingly.

"No tell-tale, Doc." Gilligan's assurance allowed me to breathe easier. "Aside from down 'ere, this baby has only two places to go, street level and the top."

Conversation ceased as the cracksman activated the lift, which rose to our destination.

We stood in the darkness of the reception area while Gilligan, aided by the bullseye, made a rapid survey of the entire suite of offices. Upon his return, the news was good.

"It's a safe go," he stated, activating a lamp on the reception desk. "The blinds is drawn and no light will show. Especially since this whole layout is surrounded by a terrace."

"Terrace?" This had not been mentioned but, then, I had not studied the blueprints of the building.

Holmes had. "Recall that this floor was originally designed as the architect's living quarters," he said. "Wallingford, you and Watson check out the records room. It's right this way. Long shot, but there could be a master plan showing which portfolio belongs to which client."

We were walking as he spoke and the sleuth indicated a room that I recalled as housing records and research.

"Meanwhile, Slim and I will be in the conference room where, I trust, we will ferret out the hiding place of the files."

I gazed after my friend and the cracksman, quite dumbfounded. Much had been made of the secrecy surrounding the client portfolios. What prompted Holmes to be confident that they were secreted in the Conference Room? Then I recalled our trip to Waldo Wynn-Chichester's bookstore. "Of course," I thought, "that's why he wanted those original blueprints." Holmes had paced off all the rooms in the Leicester complex, and his estimate didn't agree with the dimensions listed in the blueprints for the conference room. There was missing space and that's where the files were.

Wallingford had the door to the records room open and a light on. There was a dubious air about him.

"We're in the right station but on the wrong track, Doc. Holmes said that only the big boss and the account executives know about those files. All of these cabinets are locked, but it is still a bit public for something they are so hush-hush about. Oh well, see if you can find a label marked 'confidential,' will you?"

Actually, I did find what we were looking for and

alerted the ex-confidence man who surveyed my discovery with satisfaction.

"Simple Falmouth lock . . . same type as the others." One arm indicated the room's contents as the hand of the other retreated to his trouser pocket and emerged with a well-filled key ring.

"I think I've got something that will do the trick." Selecting a small key, he attempted to insert it into the cabinet lock, but was unsuccessful. He then tried a second choice.

"Good heavens," I thought, "everyone here, save me, can defy security measures at will. Nothing is safe with the likes of Slim and Wallingford around."

After a bit of jiggling, Wallingford made the second key work and the top drawer slid open at his touch. He pushed a release slide and the other three drawers were accessible as well.

"Take the top, Doctor, and I'll start at the bottom. Let's see what we come up with."

My eyes were beginning to blur by the time I had worked my way through the second drawer and looked despairingly at Wallingford who had done the same with the other two.

"They are just making it hard for us, Doctor," said my accomplice. On his knees, he peered at the underside of the bottom drawer and repeated the process with the others. After inspecting the back of each drawer, he surrendered.

"It's not here. If we check out the rest of them, it's an all-night job. We might ask the high command for a decision."

"Sounds sensible," I replied and, somewhat crest-fallen, we rejoined Holmes and Gilligan in the conference room.

Our fellow burglars were busily engaged in what they did best. Holmes was facing the west side of the room, his right elbow resting in the palm of his left hand while his right hand supported his chin. Obviously he was in deep thought. Behind the sizeable bar, Gilligan was at the wall Holmes gazed at, the fingers of both hands outstretched and feeling their way over the surface as though miniature eyes were in the sensitive tips of each digit. The thin cracksman had abnormally long arms anyway and, pressed against the wall, arms and fingers extended, he brought to mind a huge spider poised to snare some unsuspecting prey.

Then Gilligan turned to face us.

"There's a vault of some sort back there Mr. Holmes, if you say there is, but the release catch isn't in that wall."

"We feel that three or four individuals have use of this secret place, and not infrequently either. The release mechanism would be hidden somewhere easily reached. With a client possibly waiting to go over his holdings, securing them should not take long either."

Holmes swung around, suddenly aware of our presence.

"Ah . . . any luck?"

"We drew a blank, Holmes; going through all those. . . ."

"Never mind," interrupted the sleuth. "It was a wild shot at best. If we can find. . . ."

"Here now, Gov, we're on ter somethin'."

As we turned towards Gilligan's voice, I experienced a shock. The cracksman seemed to have vanished. Then I realized that he was crouched behind the bar but a short distance from the wall he had been inspecting.

"It's a wire, Mr. 'Olmes, and that tells a story."

I made haste, along with Holmes and Wallingford, to get to where I could watch the cracksman. On his knees, he felt with one hand underneath the bar, which was supported by four legs and not in contact with the floor. I could not see what Gilligan had found, but I could view the half smile of satisfaction on his face. Rising to a half crouch, he pulled a drawer from the piece of furniture and eagerly felt inside the space made accessible.

"Yep, she runs right up so we'll just pull out this 'ere top one and see what's waitin' fer us."

The top drawer he referred to contained bottle openers, a hand juicer and other paraphernalia necessary to produce good spirits with spirits from a glass. Gilligan did not bother to look into the aperture but let his fingers roam where the drawer had been.

A barely audible metallic sound caused four heads to turn towards the wall behind. I barely suppressed an exclamation of surprise. It would have seemed unprofessional, considering my companions, though I could have pleaded a lack of experience with mechanical marvels of concealment.

A considerable portion of the wall was now about five inches closer to us. "Spring activated," I surmised. I could hear, faintly, a whirring sound, somewhat like the meshing of gears. The portion of the wall that had sprung out now slid upwards and an area running, at a guess, six feet vertically and fifteen feet wide was revealed. In rows, one atop the other, were the portfolio files. Cardboard identification slips were fitted into metal receptacles on the face of each one.

"I did send you chaps on a wild goose chase," stated Holmes as his eyes flashed from one file to the next. "Here's what we want, for a start at least." Sliding one from its resting place, he crossed to the conference table with the three of us at his side. I could see a single name, Manheim, typed on cardboard on the face. The top swung from right to left and the entire contents were revealed. Holmes stepped aside with a gesture towards Wallingford.

That veteran of many a "dodge," and inventor of a few as well, slid into a chair and pulled out the one next to him for me. I had been assigned a duty in this search for information and had sharpened pencils and a pad of paper ready. Gilligan secured a lamp from a casual table, which he placed close to us and lit, turning up its wick as he did so. The added illumination revealed impressive-looking documents, and Wallingford selected the topmost, which proved to be a group of certificates secured together. Placing them flat on the table, Wallingford smoothed out the heavy paper for a first look. Then,

with the speed of a bank teller, he riffled the edges
and spoke, but his words were directed to himself, an
articulation of his thoughts.

"Ten of them, a thousand each. Ten thousand
shares, Great Atlantic and Pacific Tea Company.
Ten figure identification number of the one, nine
series." From the corner of his eye he must have
noted my attempted scribblings on my pad, and he
waved in a negative manner.

"Don't bother, Doctor. This is the genuine
goods."

Carefully slipping one stock certificate from the
group, he held it in front of the lamp on the table,
moving it back and forth in the light. I noted the
A&P insignia bracketed by two winged angels in
what seemed to me to be Grecian gowns.

"An American company," commented Holmes,
as Wallingford placed the ten stock certificates to
one side.

"This one isn't," said the former confidence
man who now held a single certificate in front of
the lamp Gilligan had provided. "Birmingham
and Southern. Thousand shares. Number
0573701." As his fingers felt the paper, Wyndhaven's name flashed through my mind. Had not
Claymore Frisbee said that this was part of the
procedure of the deceased appraiser?

"It's the real thing, all right." Wallingford did
not, however, place the stock to one side but kept
looking at it as though a nagging thought was flut-
tering, moth-like, on the edge of his mind. Extract-

ing a thin notebook from his waistcoat, he referred to it, turning pages rapidly.

"Number 0573701," he repeated. Then his compressed lips relaxed and the ends curved upwards.

Leaning back in his chair, his head turned towards the sleuth.

"We've found something, Mr. Holmes."

"Counterfeit?" asked Holmes, but there was doubt in his voice.

"Nope. This certificate was part of the railroad's original issue, but I wouldn't try to sell it. Twenty thousand shares of Birmingham and Southern stock was part of the take when the Doncaster National Bank was robbed about three years back."

"I remember that job," exclaimed Gilligan. "They botched it a bit, but they got away. I always figured that one fer Clive Franklin"

Wallingford shrugged. "The owner of this particular stock wisely had made note of the numbers. They ran 0573701 through 20. I try to keep a record of such things, an old habit."

"How fortunate that you do," said Holmes. "The numbers were circulated, and any Birmingham and Southern certificate that appears is checked against them. Clive Franklin, if he was the culprit, didn't make much through B&S."

"Not a farthing," I stated. "I mean . . . didn't Wally here say the certificate was genuine but worthless?"

"Old chap, you can sell hot stock like that in any

major city in the world, if you know where to go, and buy it as well."

Wallingford confirmed Holmes' information. "There are fences that specialize in such traffic. They pay but a pittance of the face value, of course, and let the stock cool off a bit. Then they try to move it around. The smoothest way is right here," and he tapped the Manheim file.

"How so?" I asked, my mouth ajar. Here was an industry, completely illegal of course, which I had never heard of.

"It's not a new 'dodge,' Doctor," explained the expert on such matters. "Say I take a thousand shares of railroad stock from this portfolio. It's the real thing. I steal it, but I replace it with a thousand shares of genuine stock that I've bought for a song because it is stolen property. I sell the original stock, naturally. You can get wealthy in a short time that way. The beauty of it is that this Birmingham and Southern certificate might sit in this box for years. I'd be long gone by then."

"That's what Wyndhaven found," said Holmes with satisfaction. "I suspect there's more."

"Let's find out," replied Wallingford with gusto.

It took just short of an hour. There were two questionable items, and I carefully noted their identification numbers, but this was more a matter of form than anything else.

"The file is loaded, Mr. Holmes," said Wallingford, replacing the securities and closing the lid. "Somebody has made a real haul."

"I knows a couple of disposers. . . ." Gilligan threw a glance at the American and continued. "Fences, see, what have looked flush lately."

"The embezzler has to have a source," said Holmes in that automatic way of his that indicated another idea was uppermost in his mind. "The big question is, how far has this er . . . dodge . . . gone?"

This involved checking other boxes, and it was a long job. I was suppressing a yawn when Wallingford was finally satisfied.

"I think it is only the Manheim file, Mr. Holmes. The rest that we've gone over are clean."

"Thank heaven we uncovered . . . rather the late Wyndhaven uncovered, this scheme when he did. There is a logic to the embezzler concentrating on the Manheim box, he being in Berlin. On the average, his portfolio would be scrutinized less often than that of a client here in London."

"When you break this case, Mr. 'Olmes," said Gilligan with a sly smile, "I'm gonna be real interested in your explanation of how you got onto the caper."

Holmes chuckled. "Best that it is done without any reference to our excursion this evening."

It was not all over, of course. We had to retrieve Gilligan's livery that he had worn when posing as Lady Teasdale's driver. Slim had underdressed his costume with the dark apparel which was his trademark when there was, as he put it, "a little in-and-outing" to be done.

Then there was the matter of the great freight

door, our means of exit. It was not a sliding arrangement, but divided into two halves. The latest in Steinford locks was no bother, but an impressive wooden bar, reinforced by metal, was attached at one side of the aperture and designed to be swung into an L-shaped metal receptacle on the other. It was the old "bar the door" principle and immune to picklocks and such devices. However, Slim had an answer in the form of an long strand of very fine wire. He looped it loosely around the end of the upright bar and slipped the other end outside at the hinge area of the door section furthest from the bar. With all of us out of the basement, Slim closed the two halves of the freight door gently and then began a steady tug on the free end of the wire. We could hear the bar within moving from vertical to horizontal and then there was a jar as it fell into place. Some fiddling with the thin strand of wire, and Slim had it free and drew it through the almost imperceptible crack caused by the hinge arrangement.

With the bar in its lock position, the rest was easy. Gilligan's burglar tools went to work on the Steinford and had it relocked in short order.

There was no sign of our visit. Our forces then split, and Holmes and I walked a considerable distance before securing a hansom. Dawn tinted the eastern sky with those first faint shades of pink when we finally reached Baker Street.

10

The Watchman and Receptionist

Our nighttime excursion had been a nerve-wracking affair, and both Holmes and I made up for our early morning return by sleeping late indeed. As we combined breakfast and lunch, Holmes indicated that he had found an inner satisfaction in that a milestone in the case had been reached.

"The motive is now crystal clear, Watson. Considering the price placed on human life by our local thugs, it's enough to warrant a dozen deaths."

My resistance low, I succumbed to another delicious scone and lavishly applied butter. "You suspected the Manheim file from the start, I imagine. Obvious."

"Once established, all things become obvious."

"You did say the motive might point to the culprit?" I recalled reaching for a jar of Mrs. Hudson's homemade preserves.

"Would that the finger of guilt was more specific. The raison d'etre for Wyndhaven's death being embezzlement, we have to consider the Leicester group as our suspects. Since the tampering with the German's securities is a sophisticated bit of skullduggery, we can bypass the lower echelon of the organization."

"Leaving three account executives and the old boy himself," I stated, savoring the last of the scone topped by blueberry jam.

"Agreed. Though the receptionist, who also handles the telephone switchboard, offers possibilities. A great deal of the business of the firm must be known by one in that position."

"What now, Holmes?"

"A mite more speed, for one thing, before this matter begins to drag out. Prior to training our sights on our main targets, however, I think some words with the watchman and the receptionist are called for as we move into the second phase of our inquiries."

For unexplained reasons, Holmes wished to approach Wallace Wailes and Mabel Stark, the watchman and receptionist, on their home grounds. Wailes resided in Kensington and it was arranged for Athelney Jones to accompany us to lend an official air to the proceedings. This puzzled me. I could not recall a time when my friend had any problem questioning people without some symbol of Scotland Yard at his elbow. My query relative to this prompted a response that shed light on a different matter entirely.

"Commissioner Brickstone is playing a game,

Watson, and it serves our interests to go along with him."

"Brickstone's attitude quite overwhelmed me."

"He is doing a neat job of riding two horses. If pressed, he can state that Wyndhaven died of natural causes in his opinion but that I so strongly contended otherwise that he, unofficially, put me in charge of the case and was cooperating because of . . . shall we say . . . previous services."

Our trip to the suburb was uneventful, and we found the cottage of Wallace Wailes without difficulty. It proved to be a tidy little place with a well-tended exterior. I anticipated the presence of an active wife, or perhaps daughter, but learned that the watchman was a widower without offspring. He brewed a fine cup of tea, however, and fussed around his small living room getting us seated and comfortable.

"You'll be wanting some talk about the Wyndhaven gentleman, of course. I only saw him once that day. Once when he was alive."

Inspector Jones, having questioned the watchman already, had no new thoughts and seemed resigned to his role as window dressing.

"I'm interested in your working procedure," said Holmes. "You are employed by Leicester Ltd., not the building, am I right?"

" 'Tis the same thing, Sir. Mr. Leicester owning the building like he does. You are right though; my duties only involve the investment office."

"And no one is allowed entry without your approval."

" 'Tis a nice way you put it, Mr. Holmes, but my approval isn't worth tuppence. I'm given a list of people with appointments before we're officially open. Usually by Mabel Stark, the receptionist. Everyone that comes in I check against my list."

The watchman anticipated Holmes' next question.

" 'Course there might be somebody unexpected like, but I don't let 'em up the lift till I get clearance from the office."

"The stairs . . ." said Holmes suggestively.

"The door right beside the lift." Wailes shook his head. "There's little reason for them 'cept the building code. They are circular and steel and if you've a mind to try 'em, 'tis like walkin' up the inside of a lighthouse. Of course, if the lift took a mind to act up, they would see some usage, but none of our clients is goin' to trudge up eight floors. You can bet on that."

Holmes had maneuvered the man around to where he wanted the discussion and kept prompting him.

"We have the stairs, unused, the lift and the street door. . . ."

"That's the whole kettle of fish, Mr. Holmes. Had I designed it myself, I couldn't ha' made my job easier."

"Is there . . . ? No, there would have to be a basement."

"As tight as the main floor, Sir. Just the freight entrance and an artillery piece would have a problem with it. The building is erected on an incline so there are windows below, but they're barred fer fair."

I resolved to have no part in this discussion lest I let slip that we already had a working knowledge of said basement and other areas as well.

"You are the day man, right?" asked Holmes, intent on keeping the words flowing.

"Aye. The office is usually closed by the time my relief gets there. He's got long hours, but it's an easy go. Once the porter is finished tidying upstairs, Jake lets him out and secures the street entrance along with the door to the lift and the stairs. Then he sets up his cot and gets himself forty winks. No one could get in the street entrance without him aknowin' it."

"That's Jake Biggs, the night man," stated Jones, his notebook in evidence.

Holmes' manner indicated that he was satisfied, and his meeting with Wailes was but part of a pattern anyway. Then he made further inquiry. It was a trick that I'd seen him use before.

"I understand there are times when the office force works late."

"If there's somethin' big afoot, the whole batch are liable to stay most of the night with the phones goin' lickety-split. Jake don't get his winks then, you bet."

"We can bypass that unusual occurrence. Could you give me an idea of what happens at closing time on a normal business day?"

" 'Bout like you'd imagine, Sir. Mr. Leicester

gives 'em the 'all clear' and down they comes. Not all at once. Hoskins, the bookkeeper, usually leads the pack. I think his wife's a mite fussy about mealtimes. The secretaries, most often, are next. They are sisters and always leave together. After that, 'tis a guess, though the old man . . . Mr. Leicester . . . is usually the last. Him or Mabel Stark."

"And you check them out," stated Holmes.

"Not really, Sir. My job is to check people in. Regular like, the last to leave the office tells me and I lock up after them. I make a game of it to break the monotony. I figure out, ahead, in what order they'll come. You know, I'm quite right a few times."

Long association makes one sensitive to the feelings of others and I could tell Holmes was pleased.

"I'll make a wager you can remember how it went the day Wyndhaven breathed his last."

Wailes displayed confidence. "No trouble, Sir, it bein' so recent and all. Hoskins was first, like always, and the girls was right behind him. Mabel Stark came next. She asked if one of the street urchins what deliver things sometimes and hang 'round outside was there, and I said I'd seen a couple. She had a letter she wanted to go by hand."

My eyes locked with those of Holmes for an instant, and I knew we both suspected the destination of the letter Wailes spoke of.

"Haf a mo," exclaimed the watchman. "I forgot to mention that this here was not really normal, for Mr. Leicester let everybody off early. Come as no surprise, though, fer 'tis the slow season and there hadn't been much doin' anyways."

"Slow season?" questioned Holmes, momentarily distracted from his main line of inquiry.

"People gets habits, some they don't even know about. 'Tis this time o' year that the first thought of the holidays comes to mind, even to investors and the like. Trading volume drops suddenly, like everyone knows, and there's just no action. A day or so later and it is all back to normal."

I did not choose to reveal to Wailes that I did not know about this seasonal phenomenon and doubted if Holmes did either. I assumed the man's reference to trading volume meant the number of shares bought and sold during a day.

"Where was I?" asked Wailes.

"Mabel Stark had just left," said Athelney Jones, much to my surprise. He had been more attentive than I had imagined.

"Right on, Inspector. After her, 'twas Macy what come. Then Mr. Leicester, in a hurry. He tol' me that the appraiser was still in the office but would be down shortly. He mentioned somethin' 'bout the Board of Trade and a speech."

"What about the other account executive?" asked Holmes. "A Mr. Andrews, I believe."

"He was on vacation at the time, Sir. Just got back today, he did."

"That slipped my mind, Mr. Holmes," said Jones apologetically.

Something was troubling Wailes and he shook

his head as though to jog his memory.

"Fer the life o' me, I can't remember Mr. Weems leavin'."

"Oh," I said instinctively, "Leicester had sent him on a mission some time earlier." Then I winced inwardly. Perhaps Holmes did not want the matter of Weems going to the Grain Pit revealed, but there was no furrow between the sleuth's eyes so I judged I had not made a blunder.

"He did," replied Wailes. I could not tell if this was a statement or a question.

Holmes chose this moment to rise.

"Mr. Wailes, we have intruded on your time long enough, and I'm most appreciative of your assistance. I know Inspector Jones is as well."

As the rest of us found our feet, Holmes gave credit where it was due.

"I trust a trip to Old Bailey does not figure in your future, Wailes. If it does, I'm sure the Crown will consider you, as a witness, a welcome gift."

"That's kindly of you, Mr. Holmes, and I'll put me mind to this matter, just in case there's a little somethin' I overlooked."

Receptionist Mabel Stark lived in the Marylebone area, conveniently close to Baker Street. We made for her address directly from Kensington.

In transit, Athelney Jones asked the sleuth if our meeting with the watchman had proved fruitful, but his manner in posing the question indicated that he expected a negative answer.

"Wailes outlined the pattern that Leicester and

his group have established through the years. Helpful in that I'm sorely puzzled as to opportunity, a matter that Watson and I went over recently."

"Oh," said the inspector. It was a short answer but expressive. Jones had no idea what the sleuth was thinking of, nor did Holmes choose to explain. Rather, he shifted to another subject.

"Where did this Andrews chap vacation? The account executive that returned today."

Jones' notebook came out of his side pocket.

"Baden-Baden, Mr. Holmes."

"You've checked that out?"

"But he wasn't even in the country when Wyndhaven died."

"Correction. Someone in the Leicester organization told you Andrews was in Baden-Baden."

"Actually, it was the old man himself," admitted Jones.

"That doesn't mean he was there, you know."

Jones was shamefaced. "I'll get right on it, Mr. Holmes."

Now it was the sleuth who posed a question. "Did you learn anything else from Frontnoy Leicester?"

"It was him what wanted to learn from me. He went around the barn a bit, but he'd give a lot to know why you think Wyndhaven was murdered. I wouldn't mind knowing myself. I mean . . . young Hopkins just had a suspicion."

The inspector's voice dwindled away and there was a weighty pause. I wondered if the sleuth was going to tell him, for I had been doing some wondering about this myself.

"What I could say at this point, Jones, wouldn't stand up in court. There is a piece of solid evidence that I must find."

"Just a hint, Mr. Holmes, for I could figure it from there." In his mind, Jones was an experienced protector of the people whose talents were being stifled by a whim.

There was a suggestion of wry humor about Holmes. "This hint would have to go to Cecil Brickstone, no doubt?"

"Well, Sir, the Commissioner is my superior."

"And so the chain begins," said Holmes, as if to himself, "and one of the links might be the guilty party and, of a sudden, our bird has flown and a great deal of money with him."

"Ooops," I thought, "did he mean to say that?"

"What money, Mr. Holmes?" The inspector was teetering on the edge of the carriage seat in his eagerness.

Holmes recovered smoothly. "Surely, Jones, your expertise tells you that this affair belongs in the 'crime for gain' category."

"If it is a crime," replied Jones, much disappointed.

There was little said during the remainder of our trip to Marylebone.

Mabel Stark opened the door to her quarters clad in a well-worn dressing gown. Hairpins and face cream were much in evidence. I felt an immediate kinship with the woman since her bedroom slippers seemed as dilapidated as my own.

In my mind I began to frame apologies for our evening visit but they proved unnecessary.

"Evening, Ma'am, I'm Inspector Athelney Jones," began our cohort.

"Of course, Inspector, I thought you'd never get here."

"You were expecting me?" stammered the astonished Jones.

"For several days." Mabel Stark spied Holmes and myself and her eyes widened, more in anticipation than surprise.

"And here we have Sherlock Holmes with Dr. Watson. Come in, come in gentlemen. What did take you so long?"

Even Holmes was nonplussed as the matronly woman ushered us into her somewhat untidy sitting room and into chairs. Her manner defied resistance.

"I've had my best tea things all laid out and had begun to wonder if it was necessary." Taking a blue willowware pot from a well-polished silver tray, she made for what I assumed was the kitchen.

Holmes speared Athelney Jones with a questioning look.

"Did someone arrange a meeting . . .?" he began.

"Nonsense." Mabel Stark's voice admonished us from beyond a door. "Obviously you think that dear Mr. Wyndhaven met with foul play. The papers say so. Well, suspicions have to be investigated, don't they? Where better to start than with me? I am the receptionist and handle the switchboard at Leicester's. Like the novels say, I'm a key figure."

The lady returned with a steaming pot and I winced. I'd had at least two cups while with Wailes and a bumpy carriage ride from Kensington. I was wondering how to put it to Mabel Stark about her facilities but dismissed that thought. For all I knew, the lady might have rinsed some of her undergarments and have them hanging there. Too embarrassing to consider. As I crossed my legs with determination to weather it out, Holmes gave indications of partial recovery from our singular welcome.

"Key figure. I said that very thing to Dr. Watson, but a few hours ago, Miss . . .?"

Receiving a nod, he continued. "Miss Stark, you must forgive us . . ."

"Yes. Yes. Yes," interrupted our hostess impatiently. "Cream?"

There were three negative gestures.

"One lump or two?"

"None, thank you Ma'am," answered Jones.

"Nor I," said Holmes. I just shook my head.

Miss Stark poured. "Now I've gone over the whole matter in my mind and figured out the points that are relevant."

"Oh my," I thought to myself, "the last thing Holmes wants are prepared answers"

The matter of answers did not arise.

"On the day in question," began Miss Stark, for all the world as if she was addressing judge and jury, "I received a cable from the Manheim offices in

Berlin. After informing Mr. Leicester, I called the Inter-Ocean Trust and told the gentleman who had contacted us that the matter had been cleared. Mr. Wilberforce, at the bank, wondered if two o'clock would be satisfactory for the appraisal and I said it was, for Mr. Leicester had instructed me to take care of the matter. We had nothing else on the books, it being the slow period. As it happened, Mr. Macy was on a client call and Mr. Leicester was at an important meeting when that dear Mr. Wyndhaven arrived. Mr. Weems had just returned, however . . ."

"Weems wasn't in the . . ." began Holmes, to no avail, for our hostess preferred to finish her train of thought without interruption.

"Mr. Weems had been in the field investigating a machine tool company in Brixton. He is our best growth situation man."

"Growth . . .?" This time my friend got in but one word.

"Mr. Weems is very good at judging the future potential of new companies. He'd been in Brixton for the better part of two days and was going to prepare a detailed report for Mr. Leicester. I had to call him away from that. He didn't know about the Manheim matter, but somebody had to attend to Mr. Wyndhaven. Then our employer returned. There was something on his mind, and he conferred with Mr. Weems for a moment and then went into the visitor's office to tend to Mr. Wyndhaven himself. Which he did. Mr. Leicester then made a cou-

ple of calls from his office through the switchboard.
He has a private line but not many people have the
number, and he likes to keep it open because . . .
well, because he likes to."

I noted that Holmes seemed about to ask a question and prayed that he would not. "Just let her talk,
Holmes," I thought to myself, "and perhaps we can
get out of here." I squirmed in my seat and un-
crossed my legs.

"Then Mr. Leicester came out of his office and
told me we could all leave early and he would see to
things. I informed the rest . . ."

At this point Mabel Stark paused for the first
time.

"I don't recall seeing Mr. Weems. . . ."

"He went . . ." I began and then subsided as the
lady fixed me with a gimlet eye.

"Everybody began to go. Then that dear Mr.
Wyndhaven opened the door of the visitor's office.
He realized that I was leaving and he asked me if I
would have a letter delivered for him by hand. He
gave me an envelope and five pence, which I thought
was too much, really, but I said I'd be glad to take
care of it. He went back to the visitor's office and I
went down in the lift. There were several of the
street urchins who hang around the building hoping
for odd jobs, and I selected the most dependable and
sent Mr. Wyndhaven's message on its way.

"Now gentlemen, if you've finished your tea, I am
a working woman and must retire for the night. I
trust I've been of assistance."

Mabel Stark herded the three of us to her door in her authoritative manner. The thought of H. Rider Haggart's "She" came to mind. As we mumbled goodnights, she delivered a parting shot.

"The only thing at all strange about the entire day was the fact that dear Mr. Wyndhaven would send a letter addressed to Mr. Sherlock Holmes."

The door slammed in our faces.

"Blimey!" whispered Jones.

"What an amazing woman," said the sleuth.

"Holmes, could we just get back to Baker Street?" I pleaded through clenched teeth.

Because of the hour, further investigation of the facts surrounding the death of James Wyndhaven was impractical. Our leave-taking of Athelney Jones was but a matter of a moment. Before Holmes could suggest a stroll home, I had hailed a hansom, directing the driver to 221B Baker Street with all possible speed. My friend's mind, much caught up with the information supplied by Wailes and the virtual monologue of Mabel Stark, must have detoured to the matter of his staid, middle-aged companion seemingly transformed into a nervous, impatient individual. Our trip was a short one and Holmes had his key ready and the door open in a trice. Thoughtfully, he paused for a word with Billy, awaiting our arrival as was his custom, whilst I made a beeline for the stairs leading up to our chambers.

Whatever had occurred to Holmes, like a true English gentleman he made no reference to it. When

I rejoined him in our sitting room, he reverted to the subject which had been uppermost on our minds for the past days.

"What did you make of our cooperative watchman and forceful receptionist, Watson?"

"That should be my question, Holmes. Since you ask, they corroborated one another along with the version Leicester gave us yesterday."

A thought coaxed a chuckle from Holmes. "Wailes brought up the message, our introduction to this whole affair. I wondered if Mabel Stark would make mention of it since doing so would reveal that she took a peek at the addressee."

"Why? She might have indicated that she respected Wyndhaven's privacy and took no heed of the destination of the message."

"Would either of us have believed her?"

"No," I conceded. "Surely an insignificant point. Can we get to the heart of the matter? Did you learn anything?"

"Yes, but more important, a possibility was suggested that could solve the matter of 'opportunity.'" Holmes was gazing at our ceiling and his voice had that removed sound, indicating that his mind was racing far ahead of his words to me.

"Opportunity." I almost choked on the word. "Good heavens, that is the key to the whole matter. For the life of me, I cannot imagine how any one of our suspects had the chance to do Wyndhaven in. With the exception of Leicester, that is."

The sleuth's mind and his eyes returned to me.

"The idea that the appraiser might have been dead before Leicester left his place of business. It is a tidy solution, I'll give you that."

"But you don't like it."

"Let's say I have not abandoned it, Watson."

One of England's finest amateur boxers was adept at sidestepping, and he well knew that I was trying to draw him out. Experience told me that I was not going to succeed.

"What is the next move, Holmes?"

"Convenience dictates that we make contact with our remaining suspects tomorrow, and one trip will do it."

"The account executives all being at Leicester Ltd.," I said. "That done, we'll have covered the lot." I could not resist one more try at worming some information out of my evasive companion.

"Do you sense that we are closing in, Holmes?"

"I have the feeling that instead of asking questions, we will be in a position to provide answers," admitted the sleuth; and that was all I could get from him.

11

Suspects and Motives

We both slept late the following morning and enjoyed a leisurely breakfast. Holmes felt that our investigation at the financial house had best be done after the main business of the day was completed.

He had cabled Frontnoy Leicester and, when we arrived at his offices the following afternoon, we found him disposed to assist us. The shrewd financier must have realized that things had gotten beyond the point where he could just wish the whole matter away. The newspapers had kept the story alive with no end of veiled references, and I felt their next contention would be that the appraiser's death had been the result of an Irish plot. They had kept their journalistic skirts clean enough, however, to go whichever way the cat jumped. Either Holmes was right or he wasn't, and our tabloids were ready to claim victory in either case. Leicester harbored the devout hope that the sleuth was in error and that death by design had not chosen his offices as a showcase. Time was on his side for, if Holmes did not come up with a solution soon, an ennui regarding the fatality would develop, for such is the path followed by the public mind. "Tell us now or tell us not at all," cries Percy Q. Public; a philosophy strongly endorsed by our press with their abhorrence of yesterday's news.

The elder statesman of the investment fraternity had made his account executives available for what Holmes termed "a discussion," and anticipated that we wished it on an individual and not a group basis. This was pleasing but it became immediately apparent that Leicester thought he was to play an active part. This could have been because he wished to relate Mr. Holmes' methods to that devoted reader of my stories, his wife. It was far more likely that Leicester felt his presence would safeguard his interests by curbing conversation regarding the firm's methods or some past occurrence not suitable for an outsider's ears. This impasse of the moment called for the use of Holmes' more than considerable diplomacy, a polished weapon the sleuth held ready for moments of need. Holmes wheeled it out with his effective prologue of confidentiality.

"My associate, Watson, and I would be dullards," he said, "if we did not recognize the advantage of your presence. A trained mind is always an asset, and you could well serve as the prod for a lagging memory. However, there is a drawback. When attempting to look at facts from another's point of view, I try to get them talking, to approach points of interest by an indirect route. Mine is not the manner of a Prosecutor for the Crown. Each of your account executives will be constrained regarding any subject touched on. If an opinion comes to mind, the question of whether the boss will approve accompanies it. What should be reasonably brief meetings might well drag out interminably."

Holmes was telling Leicester exactly what the old man intended to do and placing him in the position of having to argue against it. I had the sudden thought that a parallel might further entangle the old boy, and what I had in mind was quite true.

"This very situation is one I face often," I stated.

"You?"

I'd surprised Leicester—a good thing—and plunged ahead.

"Holmes frequently makes contact with certain members of society who are not on friendly terms with the authorities. I try to absent myself with such encounters, for they speak more freely without the presence of a biographer."

Our two-on-one effort proved successful, for Leicester could come up with no argument that would sound reasonable. I could tell that it went against his grain, but he accompanied us to the door of his office, indicating that of Harland Macy, his senior account executive. On our right was the reception desk manned by Mabel Stark, who paid us no heed. To our left was the visitor's office, Wyndhaven's last port of call while among the living. I saw Weems disappearing through a door on the other side of the large reception area. I had noted his name on the glass while waiting for my patient, Lady Teasdale, to finish her trumped-up business when I had appeared at Leicester Ltd. as a doctor and not as the associate of the world's greatest detective.

The offices of Andrews and Macy were through an archway and close on to the conference room of fond memory. The driving force of the investment house told us that he would be available if needed and sounded a bit grumpy as he did so. It occurred to me that he would feel much worse if he knew that his name was on our list of suspects.

Harland Macy was a small man, thin, with angular features and iron-gray hair sprinkled with white, like rice thrown at a wedding. It was obvious that he had been awaiting our arrival and, as is so often the case in matters of this sort, he was eager to tell us that he did not know Wyndhaven well nor could he imagine what information he might be able to give.

Holmes' response was standard and had the familiar ring of oft-used words.

"This meeting is rather a matter of procedure, Mr. Macy. You've been questioned by Inspector Jones, naturally."

Macy nodded, indicating that he had.

"He, also adhering to form, inquired as to your movements after leaving the office on the day that Wyndhaven died."

"I believe I have what the novelists refer to as 'the cast-iron alibi.' I did not go home but met my wife at the Vanguard where we dined with friends. Another married couple named . . ."

"No matter," interrupted Holmes, with an up-raised palm and a smile. "There is one area, unre-lated to the deceased, where you could assist us. I'm interested in the manner of doing things here. Those same novelists refer to 'getting the feel,' I believe."

He seemed to have struck a chord here, and I sensed that Macy was a reader of escapist literature.

"I understand, Mr. Holmes." One wrist flipped in an unconscious gesture, and the man seemed searching for a starting point.

"For instance, do you handle a certain percentage of the clients or do you specialize in some way?" asked Holmes.

"Mr. Leicester splits the clients up so the work load is more or less even, but I'm the ultra-conserva-tive arm, you might say. My people are income con-scious. It's the dividends that catch their eye, being of my vintage you see. Though we try to deny it, autumn does roll around."

This seemed as good a time as any to make the contribution that Holmes had suggested.

"One of your clients is a patient of mine. Lady Teasdale."

"Really, you've known her for some time?"

"Indeed. I was with her the other day when she came here to confer with you."

"Of course, Doctor. Now I remember."

He didn't at all, having scarcely glanced at Wal-lingford and myself, but that was of no importance.

"Let me use her ladyship as an example, gentlemen. That way I'm not revealing confidences. It is no secret that she is . . . er . . . comfortably situated."

"To say the least," I agreed.

"The late Sir Basil was very astute and her ladyship has an innate shrewdness. Her overall plan, investment goal if you will, is safety. Preservation of capital."

"The continuance of a good thing?" suggested Holmes.

"Exactly. If her income from dividends and other sources equals her expenditures, the financial picture is unchanged. All she has to fear is inflation, and the pound sterling has been remarkably stable for some years.

"Occasionally, her ladyship hears of something offering a spanking return, and I have to point out the risk factor. My job is to keep her in good, secure investments. Australian bonds at 7% and the like."

Since Holmes had routed the discussion away from Wyndhaven's death, to Macy's surprise and relief, the account executive became quite loquacious.

"That sort of account is my function now. My years give a sense of security to clients, most of whom are in my age bracket or older. But it wasn't always thus."

I knew that Holmes was grateful that Frontnoy Leicester was not present, for Macy's manner indicated a confidence.

"I've been with the firm longer than the rest. In

the old days we used to have some high times. I
helped my employer with his idea of 'The Leicester
Letter.' "

Finding no recognition on our faces, Macy was
eager to elaborate on what may have been one of his
last big moments.

"Most investment firms send out a monthly mail-
ing to their clients with recommendations, etc. It is a
promotional device. The old man was never one for
doing it like the others. Usually twice, possibly only
once a year, the Leicester Letter is released. It con-
tains no more than two messages, like 'Divest yourself of British Railways.' Or, 'Buy Canadian Wheat
Futures.' "

"This terse communique produces results?"
questioned Holmes, well knowing that it would, of
course.

"The phones start going at all hours, Mr.
Holmes, with buys and sells. You see, our people . . .
clients . . . don't have to dig their securities out of the
bank. An order by phone or cable and it is done. For
cables each client has an identifying word so that we
know it is on the up and up."

"And the Leicester Letter still exists?" queried
the sleuth.

"Oh yes. I don't function much with it anymore,
since it mostly deals with growth situations. That's
Weems' specialty. Andrews concentrates on commodities. Futures and that sort of things."

Macy's thin lips assumed a sour expression.
"When I started, we didn't have such goings-on, but

it has become big. I have to admit it."

Holmes edged the conversation back to the reason for our presence.

"What kind of portfolio is Manheim's?"

Immediately Macy took refuge behind procedure. "That's Weems' department, for he's the account executive in charge."

There was a silence which Holmes did not break, and finally the man reconsidered.

"Of course, it's common knowledge, not just here but on the street. Manheim's holdings are entirely growth oriented. Dividends don't interest him. He has bought a slice of the future, and very profitable it can be if you are right as little as thirty percent of the time."

"Why would Manheim have a portfolio of securities here? The entire German banking fraternity would be more than willing to carry out his least command?"

Macy chuckled, something rather rare for him I suspected.

"It's partly psychological, similar to what we call the gold obsession. Where do you think the largest amount of gold is, Mr. Holmes?"

The sleuth turned his palms upward indicating that this matter had not crossed his mind. "The Vaults of the Bank of London?"

"Spoken like a true Britisher and there's a lot there, for a fact. But nothing near like what's in France and not in any banks either. It is buried in the back yards of half the houses in the provinces.

They have had foreign troops on their soil more than once. In a national emergency only gold talks and the French are conditioned to be prepared."

"Germany has had some invasions themselves," commented Holmes.

"The German mind works differently. Manheim keeps the Berlin financial houses busy, but he's also got accounts in Switzerland, Hong Kong, Rio de Janeiro and here at Leicester's. If forced to flee, he has a number of places to go and ample assets when he gets there."

"I doubt that Herr Manheim anticipates leaving his native land," stated Holmes with a knowing smile.

"So do I, but to use a poker expression, he has aces up his sleeve, just in case."

"And Weems has charge of his holdings?"

"Along with the old man."

"Can they make any changes in the portfolio?"

"As long as they have a good reason and follow the general plan. Manheim has his fingers in a cross-section of industry. Let's say that Armstrong-Sidley loses a big contract and takes a dip. Mr. Leicester might pick up a block of their stock and sell some or all of the Vickers in the portfolio. Manheim still has a position in armaments; he's just switched companies with a possible profit as well."

Since Holmes seemed satisfied, Macy asked the obvious.

"Whom would you like to see next?"

"Who is closest?" replied Holmes, displaying unusual practicality.

Macy picked up the phone on his desk and after a moment, spoke into it.

"Mabel, ring Mr. Andrews for me please. Hello . . . Andrews . . . Mr. Holmes and Dr. Watson would . . . all right, right away." Hanging up, Macy summoned a smile, a muscular action that he had brought into play with Lady Teasdale.

"He's expecting you, gentlemen."

"Our thanks for your help," said Holmes and we made our way to the office next to Macy's.

Andrews had a small valise of the type known as a rucksack on his desk, which he abandoned to make us welcome. He was clean-shaven with a complexion that was almost olive. He had soft, curious-looking eyes. Like all those at Leicester Ltd., he was well turned out, though his studs were somewhat large for my taste. Still youngish, he had remained slim and, for one of medium height, he had quite long legs.

When we were seated, he returned to his desk indicating the object on it. "Going over the equipment, gentlemen, before tucking it away till spring."

"Equipment?" I asked. Holmes merely raised his eyebrows.

"I was a runner during my university days. Now I'm a volunteer with the Greater London Track and Field Organization."

Andrews could see what I was about to ask and beat me to it with a hearty laugh.

"No, no Doctor, I don't participate. Heavens, I

haven't trained for years and have all the bad habits." He flipped a pack of Melachrino cigarettes from the kit on his desk. Holmes also smoked American cigarettes, a Virginia blend supplied through the good offices of Francis Hay Moulton.*

Andrews continued. "There are times when, if we get off work a little early, we can make an afternoon meet that's not too far. We act as judges, timekeepers, starters for the runners, whatever's needed. Keeps us sort of in the swing of things and Mr. Leicester approves. Good for youngsters, you know. Playing fields of Eton and all that."

"You mentioned 'we,' " said Holmes.

"Weems, of course. Rather thought you knew. He was a top drawer miler for Ellendale in his day. Came within an ace of making the All-England Team, you know."

"No, I didn't," admitted the sleuth.

"Possibly track and field isn't your cup of tea, Mr. Holmes. Anyway, Weems and I do what we can and I keep the necessary available during the season. Towel, whistle, stop watch, blank pistol."

"Oh," said Holmes quietly. "Does this equipment serve you both?"

"No. Weems has his own kit."

"Why a blank pistol . . . ?" I began and then supplied my own answer. "Of course, to start the runners."

"Quite right, Doctor," was Andrews' answer and he twirled a small, nickel-plated revolver around

---

*The Adventure of the Noble Bachelor.

one finger before returning it to his kit. "I use Boxer Blanks myself. Fifty to a box so they last out the season."

Andrews fastened his rucksack and placed it alongside of his desk.

"Now gentlemen, what can I tell you?"

The man did not seem at all nervous about our visit nor had he made mention of how little informed he was regarding James Wyndhaven. Holmes chose his time-tested, oblique approach anyway.

"We just had an interesting discussion with your associate about the securities business."

Andrews nodded. "One of the old guard, Macy. Makes it a practice to never buy stocks or bonds himself. That used to be an unwritten law on the street. Rather wish it still was, for one is tempted to take a flyer when a situation looks particularly promising."

"How well I know," I groaned instinctively.

"You into things, Doctor?" asked Andrews with sudden interest. "Perhaps I can suggest. . . ."

"Dr. Watson's promising situations are associated with horseflesh," said Holmes drily.

"Well, there's the Albermarle Stakes next weekend." The account executive regarded me inquisitively. "Thinking of making it?"

"Certainly like to," I replied with enthusiasm, for my personal button had been pushed. "Particularly favor Sarafan."

Andrews shook his head. "Those are long odds, Doctor."

"I know but the two-year-old is untested and by Nuriana, the top stallion at Mayswood Stud. Holmes and I were there on a case—a year ago, I would say—and take my word, Nuriana is a splendid beast."*

Andrews scribbled on a notepad. "Sarafan, you say. Sounds like a rather good tip to me. I intend to be there for the running."

"You two have certainly found something in common," said Holmes.

"Rather like you and the old man, eh Mr. Holmes?"

"I don't follow. . . ."

"Come now, Sir, one of the triumphs of Leicester Ltd. was the way the old boy walked around the Netherland-Sumatra Company, and it was you who uncovered the colossal schemes of that Baron Maupertuis chap."

"I did have something to do with the matter," admitted Holmes, a statement so uncharacteristically modest as to make me despair.

"Holmes, you'll give this young chap a false impression," I cried.

My eyes swung to Andrews. "When Holmes broke the case, I caught up with him at the Hotel Dulong in Lyons. Would you believe that his room was literally ankle-deep with congratulatory telegrams. All of Europe was ringing with his name."

"I can imagine," stated Andrews. His soft eyes

---

*Sherlock Holmes and The Sacred Sword.

had widened with excitement.

"Maupertuis would have been exposed eventually," murmured Holmes in a self-deprecating manner, but I could tell that he was pleased.

"And dragged half the investment houses of Europe down with him," stated Andrews.

"How was it that your employer sidestepped the blandishments of the Baron?"

"That I don't know, but the same can be said for other things around here."

"How so?" When Holmes had his man going, his interjections were brief.

"Mr. Holmes, we do much the same work as other investment houses. Do it a little differently perhaps, but that's not the point. It is the Leicester Letter that is our principal claim to fame. One went out, you know, in '87—'Don't buy Netherland-Sumatra.' He was right. Suppose a letter went out tomorrow saying 'Buy British Wickets.' The phones would start ringing and we'd be swamped. It would spread, of course, through the whole market."

Quite taken by this, I posed the obvious question. "What if he was wrong?"

"That keeps us on the hot seat around here," admitted Andrews. "However, the boss has an edge. When it comes down to the now or the never, as it must before a Leicester Letter goes out, we have only one vote and that's Mr. Leicester's. There's an old adage which most investors accept: 'Never buy at the low or sell at the high.' "

"I don't follow this," I was forced to admit.

"Of course not," replied Andrews, but he had the good grace not to sound patronizing. "Take a big house, like Templeton and Storm. One of their bright boys comes in with something that looks good. Low price earnings ratio, valuable assets only listed at cost on their books, or any one of a number of things that would seem to indicate that the company has been overlooked. It takes about three meetings to discuss the matter at Templeton and Storm before they are ready to take a position. By that time we might have been in and already out of the stock. T&S have good people; it is just a matter of mechanics."

"Most interesting," said Holmes and, to my amazement, he began to rise from his chair. Andrews shared my surprise.

"But, Mr. Holmes, we haven't even mentioned James Wyndhaven."

"I'm sure Jones or someone else from the Yard has spoken to you about that," replied the sleuth with a smile. "I'm merely trying to capture the pattern of things around here. Do let us get off your hands and back to business. By the way, how was it in Baden-Baden?"

"Top drawer, Mr. Holmes."

"You might check up on that horse, you know . . . what was the name, Watson?"

"Sarafan."

"Might place a few pounds on her myself," stated the sleuth as we left the office of Andrews.

In the hallway, I could not restrain myself.

"Holmes, how did you know Sarafan is a filly?"

"I keep track of your markings in those racing sheets we subscribe to, Watson. I might add that I'm constantly amazed at how you manage to lose so consistently."

"But I don't wager anymore. Those are just bets with myself."

"Piffle. The money is of no importance. It is the winning that counts."

That little exchange I resolved to remember, word for word, since it summed up Holmes' philosophy better than anything else that comes to mind. With Holmes, it was never the gain, it was the game.

Now, of course, I was anxious to learn if said game was progressing.

"Did any of that talk give you a thought?"

"Indeed. There was certainly one kernel of wheat midst all the chaff." My friend regarded me with that half smile that came with his knowing an explanation was required.

"You recall young Hopkins produced a half-smoked cigarette which had supposedly fallen on the appraiser's tie when he died?"

I nodded.

"It was a Melachrino."

I indicated the door we had just left. "The same brand that. . . ."

"Exactly. Come now, old chap, we have but Weems to cover and our job is done. This next interview should be a short one."

So it proved to be.

I had seen Weems before. Like his contemporary, Andrews, he was youthful looking. His brown tweed suit was well cut to his trim figure. He had bright black eyes and a small, black moustache. There was a dead, white streak in his hair, over his left temple.

The account executive seemed anxious to help in whatever way he could. As Holmes got the conversation rolling, I realized that most of what the chap had to say was old hat to us by now, and my mind wandered a bit, considering what had been accomplished during this excursion.

Holmes must have felt that the appraiser's death was tied up in some manner with the mechanics of running the investment house. He was like a prospector panning for gold, sifting through conversational gravel and sand for the bright gleam of a fact that could fill an empty space in the mosaic forming in his mind. I knew my friend too well not to be conscious of the fact that he had struck pay dirt, though the only item that was significant to me was the matter of the cigarettes that Andrews smoked. The rest had seemed but a crash course in securities dealings, some of which sounded like as much of a gamble as my transactions with certain London bookies a while back.

"I had things rather well sorted in my mind, Mr. Holmes," Weems was saying, "upon my return to the office. I intended to dictate a rough draft on the Brixton Company to one of our secretaries, but Mabel Stark buttonholed me about Wyndhaven. I identified myself to the gentleman and was about to get him the Manheim file when Mr. Leicester arrived and took charge. He wanted me to make tracks for the commodity exchange and try and place an order for him before closing."

"Leicester spoke to us about that," said Holmes. "This commodity exchange closes rather early, does it not, for I understand you were unsuccessful?"

"If you wish to deal in futures there are but two places, London and Chicago. When we close, the Chicago people open . . . difference of time you see. This arrangement makes a commodity deal possible for the greater part of the twenty-four hours in a day. It is important when you consider that orders come from all over the world."

"Amazing," I said. "I had no idea that all this was going on, you see."

Weems smiled thinly. "Nothing for the faint-hearted, Doctor." His face suddenly sobered. "Forgive me. Considering that poor Wyndhaven chap, that remark wasn't in very good taste. I mean that commodity futures is a form of trading mainly for the high rollers. Fortunes can be made or lost in a matter of minutes."

"Following Mr. Leicester's orders, you left for the er . . . Grain Pit, I believe he said?"

"Yes, Mr. Holmes. I was able to secure a carriage promptly, and the driver did his best, but we couldn't make it by the closing bell. I telephoned Mr. Leicester and took off for my digs. Actually, I spent the rest of the day doing my report on the Brixton Company at home on my own machine."

"Yes, Leicester had given you the afternoon off, hadn't he?" Holmes pondered a moment, then shifted from the world of finance.

"Your co-worker, Andrews, was gathering his track and field equipment when we spoke to him. . . ."

"He's just getting to that?" asked Weems. "I took my stuff home weeks ago. Nothing doing till late spring, you see."

"The matter of your accomplishments during university days came up," continued Holmes. "Watson's interest in runners is confined to the four-legged variety, and I'm not up on that sort of thing at all. What was your event?"

"The mile. In my third year I was also anchor man on our relay team." Weems' black eyes held a far-off look for a moment. "That was the year we won the Midlands Meet hands down." He shook his head. "Past history."

Noting that Holmes had extracted the golden cigarette case that the King of Bohemia had given him, Weems searched the room with his eyes.

"I've an ash tray around somewhere, Mr. Holmes." He opened a drawer of his desk, but Holmes forestalled a search.

"Please don't bother, for we've leaving anyway." The sleuth made small talk as we all rose.

"Andrews said that you almost made the All-England Team."

The smile on Weems' face had a bitter tinge to it. "I do think that's one of the most distasteful words in our language, 'almost.' "

As we left the man's office, Holmes headed for the lift, evidently feeling that another go at Frontnoy Leicester would serve no purpose. He had been quite lackadaisical in his encounters with the account executives but now seemed in haste. Once removed from the building, I sounded the first note of my familiar cantata, to learn if my friend was of a revealing frame of mind.

"That Weems fellow . . . struck me as being a mite deep. Doesn't smoke either. A neat touch there, Holmes."

"You give evidence of deep waters yourself, Watson. Was I that transparent?"

"Certainly not. I have seen you in action before, you know."

We were able to secure a four wheeler, which Holmes directed back to Baker Street.

"As I recall Macy's office, don't think he smokes either," I continued suggestively.

"Leicester does. Watson, I did mention that I knew how Wyndhaven was killed, but did not know in what manner, did I not?"

"A more mystifying remark, I cannot conceive."

"You have a point. To me, the appraiser's death was either premeditated and planned or it was an act of the moment, an improvised homicide."

"I'll wager you've learned which?" This turned out to be an inspired guess.

"Yes. Rather important, you see. So much so that we have but to tidy up a few loose ends before entering this affair in the case book."

I often felt that Holmes took a delight in astonishing me and he certainly succeeded this time. Then, before I could recover, he perversely turned to another subject.

"You mentioned seeing me in action, which prompts a question I've been meaning to ask you. Have you been tiptoeing off to one of those gun clubs, Watson?"

Ah hah, I thought, he's still chewing over our battle in the streets. When puzzled, my friend stuck to a thing with the persistence of a bulldog. But I had learned a bit about evasion through the years and decided to put it to use.

"Gun clubs, you say? Well, I have given up those expensive trips to Thurston's for billiards, you know."

Holmes chose to treat this as an affirmative to his question and it pleased him, coming as an antidote for nagging doubts.

"Sensible, really. Had I fallen heir to the weapon of a living legend, I might well decide to become proficient with it. Do continue your practice, old fellow, for we might not be here now but for your aptitude."

The encouraging smile on my friend's face suddenly vanished as a new thought occurred.

"I wonder why I didn't think of that before. The morning after Wyndhaven's death, an attempt was made on both our lives. Since then, not a move has been made against us."

"Well, Holmes, we did rather bag the bunch that was after us."

"There are more of the same breed, readily available for hire. No, it is obvious what happened."

"I'm glad to hear that." I fear my tone was testy.

"When the story broke in newsprint, our adversary suspected that we knew about the Manheim file."

"All the more so after the visit of that bogus lawyer, Straithway."

"But there was no˙ hue and cry. Leicester must have gone over the German's portfolio. Only sensible thing to do, but to him, it seemed in order. Now we were not dangerous to the murderer."

"Quite an error on someone's part, Holmes, if you have solved the case."

"I would say so," was his reply and there was that thinly disguised smugness about him that always succeeded in getting my dander up a bit.

This discussion was terminated by our arrival at 221B, nor did it continue when we reached our chambers for we had company.

Slim Gilligan and Wallingford's presence did not surprise me, for I had been wondering what they had been up to. With them was a small, sandy-haired man with a bland face. There was nothing about his features or clothing that would prompt attention and one would be hard pressed, if asked, to describe him. He was Slippery Styles, the human shadow. I knew that someone, unwittingly, had acquired a constant companion. If Holmes wished anyone followed, Styles was the man he called for. The sleuth contended that Slippery could follow a sinner into hell without getting his coat singed.

"So," I thought, "another of 'the rag-tag army' has been in the field. For what purpose, I wonder?"

Following greetings, that question was answered.

"What luck, gentlemen?" asked Holmes, as he stoked the aged brier, that he sometimes fancied, with shag.

"No lack of it," replied Wallingford. "Andrews was easy."

"Money?" inquired the sleuth.

"Right on, Mr. Holmes. He's just keeping his head above water."

"Watson and I spoke with the man but a short while ago. A gambler, of course."

"And unlucky," contributed Gilligan. "He's making the bookmakers happy."

Wallingford nodded. "On top of that, he's into the futures market for fair. If corn prices drop, he could be wiped out."

"Singular," commented Holmes. "Commodities are his specialty at Leicester Ltd."

Exasperation, which so frequently haunted me, was present again. Recalling Andrews' remarks on this very day, it was easy to figure him for a man who liked to take a flyer. He practically said so. It was equally simple to realize that Holmes had his associates checking out the third of the three M's he often mentioned. Means, method, and motive; the trio that so often led to that welcome word, solution.

"Weems was a mite trickier, Mr. Holmes," said Gilligan. "Slippery, here, gave us the handle on him."

"The man has two establishments, Mr. 'Olmes," explained Styles. "I figgers his wife thinks that Weems works late a lot at his office. That ain't the case, you see, fer he spends a lot of time at the Cartright Hotel in the company of a certain redheaded lady what's registered as Vivian Sinclair."

"Fortunately," added Wallingford, "Miss Sinclair works a bit as a photographer's model." The former confidence man handed Holmes an eight-by-ten picture, which the sleuth glanced at before passing it to me. Miss Sinclair was striking, as redheaded women so frequently are.

"There's a bit more to it," continued Wallingford. "Weems pays the rent at the Cartright, not too big an item. He lives with his wife in Mayfair where as much gossip goes on as in other localities, I'm happy to say."

I could picture, with little difficulty, two or three servant girls going about their duties with a starry look as they thought of the handsome American.

Wallingford elaborated. "Mrs. Weems is a nice enough lady but limited you might say. Not upstairs," he quickly added, tapping his forehead with one finger. "She's from the midlands and married Weems right after he came down from his university. Bit of an athletic hero, he was. Her father had some money which is probably what helped Weems get started but. . . ."

"I'm with you," stated Holmes, through a cloud of smoke. "Small town girl, no interest in or aptitude for London society."

"You've got it, Mr. Holmes. The lady is happy enough and I don't figure she's on to the Vivian Sinclair situation. It's just that Weems has gone as far as he can. The rest of the road depends on the social angle. The right parties with the right people."

"And a wife who says the right things," said the sleuth. "Weems can't make it alone and his devoted wife is now . . ."

"A drag," concluded Wallingford bluntly. "If this chap is ambitious, he must know he's come to a dead end."

"That's motive," said Holmes, nodding in approval. "Also a very detailed bit of work, lads. I'm sure Watson, in one of his overdramatized recountings, would refer to it as 'painstaking investigation.' "

"Glad you said that, Gov," was Slim Gilligan's comment, but he did not look happy. "Fact is, that's the end of our road, too."

Wallingford shared his cohort's disappointment. "Frontnoy Leicester is the clinker, Mr. Holmes. He certainly doesn't need any of the folding stuff."

"He's too old for redheads," added Slim.

"More important, he knows it," stated the American. "His backtrail is clean as can be. No skeletons lying around as far as I could learn and, if there were, they would have surfaced long before this.

He's in line for knighthood."

Holmes nodded and I noted that his eyes narrowed. "What about family?"

"Just him and the wife. There was a daughter who died in a riding accident some years back. The wife took it hard and has been a bit of a recluse ever since." Wallingford shot a glance at Slim. "The old boy puts in a full working day, every day, and gives speeches. . . ."

"Also active on the board of a lot of charities. He's what you might call a . . . paragon." Slim looked quite pleased with his description.

Holmes crossed to the mantle, leaning against it thoughtfully.

"I wouldn't worry about Frontnoy Leicester's motive," he said after a moment. "You've given me one. The man has nothing to keep him going except his business and reputation. Suppose he learned that the Manheim portfolio had been tampered with? His first thought would be that the embezzlement must be concealed. If it got out, he wouldn't have a client on his books. Even if he made restitution out of his own pocket, his business would be ruined. The Leicester Letter, his standing as the grand old man — it would all be gone."

Gilligan seemed dubious. "I don't know, Gov, murder is the big drop." He shot a quick glance at Styles, as if seeking support. "Fer an amateur, it's no easy go."

"Believe me, Slim, men have been killed for less."

"What about Leicester's senior executive, Macy?" I asked. "Has he been dismissed as a possibility?"

"That gentleman," replied Holmes, "stated that he had an iron-clad alibi, and that happens to be true. From his departure from the offices till after the discovery of Wyndhaven's body, he was in a public restaurant."

"Andrews also had an alibi . . ." I began.

"Not in Baden-Baden he don't," said Wallingford, a trifle grimly I thought.

"You mean he lied as to his vacation whereabouts?"

"It might have been more of an expediency measure, Watson," stated Holmes. "Our gambling executive was not registered in Germany, but he may well have been at some race meet and desirous of keeping that fact concealed from his employer."

"But, as of now, Andrews has no alibi?"

"None. Gentlemen, we are now at the hair-splitting stage, I believe."

From Holmes' manner, I sensed that he had evaluated all of the facts that investigation had brought his way and had made his decision. His next words confirmed this.

"All of our major suspects had a motive, but that knowledge has not affected the situation as I view it. The picture is complete and ready for framing. However, Styles, I want you and your relief men to keep watching the Sinclair woman. Just mark that to a feeling. I've arranged to have words with Claymore Frisbee, our client, and cables to Commissioner Brickstone and Leicester will not be amiss. There are some points we'll go over with them after dinner, Watson."

Slim, Wally and Slippery Styles had come to a conclusion as Holmes spoke, and it was Gilligan who voiced it.

"You've cracked it, haven't you, Gov?"

Holmes nodded. "As an unofficial body, we've gone as far as we can. As to the resolution, there are problems. It is all rather dependent on whether the Commissioner tries to play both ends against the middle or not."

The sleuth had been almost speaking to himself and now cut short his musings.

"Let's keep things operative until we learn what transpires this evening."

The boys took this as a signal for adjournment and departed. No questions were asked, even by me, for Holmes held to a practice of making his revelations to clients first. "After all, we are in business," he was wont to say.

"In a loose sense," was my habitual rejoinder, and it proved most apt regarding this affair.

My friend notified Mrs. Hudson that he would be available for dinner at six-thirty and departed for the offices of the Inter-Ocean Trust leaving me to mull over our trip to Leicester Ltd., for I was certain it was there that the sleuth had crossed his final T. At his request, I cabled Brickstone and Frontnoy Leicester that Holmes would be ready with a report on the J.W. matter at eight this evening.

During our dinner, conversation was unrelated to the case. This was not perversity on Holmes' part. Brickstone and Leicester would join us, and the sleuth hated a twice-told tale. Also, when no action was possible, he liked to disassociate himself from a subject that had been benefitting from his undivided attention.

Needless to say, my habits did not coincide with his. Finally I got in a question that had an association with the Wyndhaven matter.

"Did you bring a check or is Claymore Frisbee handling it by mail?"

"Check?" Holmes' eyes met mine with some difficulty for he well knew what I was referring to.

"I assume you revealed all to the banker, for he is our client. Made you a very liberal offer he did, and I've been wondering how you handled it."

"Actually, Watson, I could not accept the man's money."

"You what?" Surely there was a rush of blood to my face and, at the moment, I must have resembled Athelney Jones.

"I mean, Frisbee was trying to avenge his friend's death and we cannot but admire his motives. Since he had offered a fee of my choosing, I said I'd take ten pounds for expenses."

"Ten pounds! Do you realize how many men you had on this job and the time it has taken? Sherlock Holmes claiming a fee of ten pounds?"

I was so worked up about the matter that the remainder of the time before the arrival of our visitors was spent in stubborn silence as I brooded on the very loose business arrangements that were the fashion on Baker Street.

12
Off the Case

The Commissioner of Police was the first to arrive. His normally high color was even more pronounced, and he was breathing heavily, in short gasps.

"Dragged away in the middle of a party, my wife ready to bounce a vase off my skull and, as a crowning touch, I've got to trudge up the longest flight of stairs. . . ."

"Come now, Commissioner, only seventeen steps."

"Easy for you to say, Holmes, being as thin as a lathe, but you put on a bit around the middle and see how it feels. Evening Doctor."

Mopping his brow with Irish linen, Brickstone lowered himself gratefully into our Queen Anne chair. "This had better be one of your best efforts. I should accept nothing less than the solution of that Jack the Ripper nightmare."

"I can give you a solution, Commissioner, but there are complications."

Holmes' sober manner communicated itself to

Cecil Brickstone and that look — half wary, half weary — crept into his eyes.

Following a gentle knock, Billy opened the hall door.

"Mr. Frontnoy Leicester," announced our page boy, stepping aside.

If the commissioner's manner had been distraught, Leicester's was the opposite. Urbane and collected, the aged financier might have been arriving at Lord Backwater's Hunt Ball. His eyes were as revealing as those of a croupier, but there was about him a sense of malicious satisfaction.

"A strange time for a meeting and an inconvenient one," he said, nodding to the rest of us. "However, I would have traveled to Zanzibar for the sheer pleasure of hearing the great Sherlock Holmes apologize."

"I hadn't intended to include that in the evening's entertainment," said Holmes.

"But you will, Sir, for 'tis the only sporting thing to do. This matter would have been over and done a week ago but for your stubborn obsession. Now the journals have enjoyed a field day, but your admiring public has been waiting for your magic hat trick to no avail. I'm glad that I decided to give you rope. I must say you baffle me, Holmes. For an investigator of some fame, you seem to have completely overlooked that indispensable you chaps are always prattling about. I refer to motive."

"I can produce motives for you, in wholesale lots." There was that quality in Holmes' voice that alerted me as to who was being given enough rope.

"This I must hear," snorted Leicester. "It is said you've been making much of a cigarette in the lips of a man who did not smoke and some missing notes, but it's not enough. I knew Wyndhaven better than most, and he was one of those rare ones without enemies. If the chap was done in, it would have to relate to the Manheim portfolio, which I went over carefully. All the others as well, and a devilishly long job it was. All because of you, Sir. Now, do pull your rabbit out of the hat, for the Commissioner and I are all ears."

"You found the Manheim file completely in order?"

"I did. No tampering there and no counterfeit to have sent Wyndhaven into a tizzy. After close to a lifetime, I know authentic stocks and bonds when I see them."

"I could have saved you some trouble. You have my word that every certificate is authentic."

"How would you know that?" asked the financier. His jocular mood was slipping away as he sensed that things were not as he had pictured them.

"That is not relative. The key fact is that most of those authentic certificates you refer to are not worth their cost of printing."

Brickstone was leaning forward in his chair, his eyes intent on Holmes. Leicester's jaw dropped and then his teeth clicked together angrily. "Talk sense, man."

"Most of the Manheim portfolio consists of stolen

property. On the open market they wouldn't fetch tuppence, for their serial numbers are known and circulated."

Leicester slowly sank back in his chair, his gaze riveted to the sleuth. "Oh my god," he finally said.

"There's your motive," said Holmes. "That's what Wyndhaven discovered and why he had to be eliminated." His head swung towards Brickstone. "That's also why there are complications. If this leaks, that vital sense of security in people's minds will be shattered. There will be a minor panic that might cause a run on the market." The sleuth's cold eyes found Leicester's as he repeated a phrase of the financier. "Monkey see, monkey do."

"Oh my God," mumbled Leicester again, and there was that high note of anguish in his voice.

"As to Wyndhaven's death, the list of suspects was small and once I knew the security precautions and the timetable of those in the office, there were but two possibilities."

Leicester was shaking his head, but his heart wasn't in it. "No one could have returned, unseen, to the office to kill Wyndhaven."

"In two cases it was not necessary. For one, you had but to kill Wyndhaven and leave, telling the watchman that the appraiser was still in the office. As simple as that."

Some of the fire returned to the old man. "You cannot mean that I am a suspect. A man of my reputation? It is not to be believed."

"Suppose you had made that statement relative to

our mutual acquaintance, Baron Maupertuis?"

Leicester was obviously incapable of grasping Holmes' point.

"When I exposed the dapper Baron, lorgnettes fell all over London. There are still some ladies of fashion who are distant towards me, for they refuse to believe that Maupertuis could have been a swindler. What was it that made you wary of the Netherland-Sumatra scheme?"

Dragging his mind to another time was an effort for the old man. "There was something in the back of his eyes. It was as if he was secretly laughing at a gullible world."

"An intuitive reaction. How fortunate for Leicester Ltd. that you paid heed to your feelings and did not dismiss them with a statement like 'It is not to be believed.' "

"All right, Mr. Holmes, you've made your point." Leicester looked at Brickstone with a forced smile, devoid of humor. "So I was a suspect."

The commissioner shrugged. "I can't speak for Holmes. Our law says innocent until proven guilty, but you don't investigate a case that way." Brickstone's eyes rose to the sleuth standing at the mantle.

"What did happen? What put you on to this from the beginning?"

When I first saw the corpse. I realized that Wyndhaven had been frightened to death. The burn on his tie was made by the wad of a blank cartridge. A blank has no lead bullet and something has to keep the powder within the cartridge case, so a wad is used. It's not dangerous except if it hits one in the eye. The murderer confronted Wyndhaven in the empty office with a pistol. He probably built up the suspense by cocking the weapon and then he fired. Confronted with the prospect of death and hearing the shot was too much for the appraiser's weak heart. He died."

"What a fiendish plot," I exclaimed.

"Actually, it was an improvisation with the murderer using what means he had at his disposal. Had you, Leicester, been the culprit, you could have planned the death. You knew that Wyndhaven was coming to the office to go through the Manheim file. If it had been vital for you to silence him, you had the time to figure out the best way to do it. The actual murderer didn't have that advantage."

"Who was it?" asked Leicester.

"The only one who didn't have to come back to the office, other than yourself, to kill Wyndhaven. It was Weems."

"But he had a perfect alibi," exclaimed Brickstone. "Leicester here sent him to the commodity exchange."

"He never went," was Holmes' simple explanation. "Weems had been away from the office for two days doing a field report in Brixton. When he returned he learned, of a sudden, that Wyndhaven was in the office and was going to inspect Manheim's holdings. He was panic-stricken and trying to figure out what to do when you . . ." Holmes indicated the aged financier ". . . took the matter out of his hands. You told him, confidentially, to get over to the commodity exchange and then went into the visitor's office to greet Wyndhaven. Weems went to his office and stayed there. He couldn't leave for something had to be done about the appraiser. He was safe enough if he kept out of sight. No one would know whether he had gone to the exchange or not. All he had to do was put a call through to his employer to report that he hadn't reached the Grain Pit in time. He had been given the rest of the afternoon off, recall. Then you, Leicester, dismissed the staff and after some time came to the door of the visitor's office and told Wyndhaven to put the Manheim box in your office when finished. Weems heard this, of course, and when you left he had his opportunity. He didn't know how to dispose of the appraiser, all he knew was that the man had a weak heart. Then he had an inspiration. There was a weapon, one that could be deadly to a man with cardiac trouble. The blank pistol that was part of his equipment when officiating at track and field meets."

"But Holmes," I said, "Weems told us that he had taken his gear home at the end of the season."

"That may have been true," said the sleuth. "If so, he went to Andrews' office and took his gun. It was a brilliant spur of the moment idea."

"Risky," stated Brickstone. "It might not have worked."

"Agreed. But it did. Wyndhaven died, ostensibly from natural causes, a masquerade murder. Weems wasn't out of the woods yet. He put the Manheim file in your office, Leicester, but there were Wyndhaven's notes which could prove incriminating, so he destroyed them. Knowing the porter would appear shortly, he was hurried. The burn mark on the appraiser's tie bothered him and he had another inspiration. He went to Andrews' office and took one of the cigarettes from the pack in his fellow broker's kit." Holmes paused for a moment, glancing at me.

"That bears out your idea, Watson, that he used Andrews' pistol. In getting it, he would have seen the cigarettes."

It hadn't been my thought at all, but if it pleased Holmes to include me in his solution, who was I to say nay?

"Weems lit the cigarette and arranged it so that it would appear to have dropped from the dead man's mouth. Then he hid himself in his own office again."

Leicester's head was shaking, this time in amazement.

"A masterful recreation, but the man was trapped. How could he get out of the building unseen?"

The ends of Holmes' lips twitched. "I've done some investigation relative to that. Weems waited till the porter arrived. The man went to get his broom, dust cloth, and whatever else he uses, and Weems got into the lift. He opened the escape hatch and climbed through it to the roof of the conveyance.

When the porter found the body, he wasted no time getting down to the ground floor to notify the watchman. Both the porter and watchman dashed outside to report the death. Inspector Hopkins said that he saw both of them with the constable returning to the building. Remember, Watson?"

Actually, I didn't, but I nodded anyway.

"While they were gone, Weems got down into the lift and out the front door undetected. He must have blessed his lucky star, for he had committed a murder that didn't seem like one and made a seemingly impossible escape as well."

The commissioner's smile of satisfaction had a certain grimness about it. "His luck ran out when Hopkins got suspicious and you appeared on the scene, Holmes. We shall deal with Mr. Weems."

"A moment," said the sleuth. "I have reason to believe that he is planning to jump it. To bail out after he's worked his scheme as much as he can."

"So?" asked Leicester, who suddenly seemed ten years younger.

"He must have the money that he secured from Manheim's securities hidden somewhere. It might be advisable to locate that before closing in on Weems. It is the only real evidence you have."

"Brickstone, here, and his men can surely handle that," stated Leicester. "All they say about you is true Mr. Holmes, for you have indeed pulled the rabbit out of the hat. Now the official sinews of the law can take charge."

I was appalled that the old hypocrite could get the

words out. It was so evident that, with the case solved, Leicester wanted to get Holmes out of the way. He was figuring on making some sort of a deal with the commissioner so that the theft of a client's property from his supposedly impregnable offices would be covered up.

Brickstone, still riding two horses, seemed to fall in with this.

"Magnificent, Holmes," he said, shaking the sleuth's hand enthusiastically. "I'll have the boys sweep up all the pieces. I'd better get to it right now."

"Here, I'll go with you," cried Leicester, and Holmes and I were left staring at each other.

"Why the old goat," I exclaimed. "A moment ago he was a pitiful, broken man. Now you've saved his bacon and he's off with a few words of approval."

Holmes was actually chuckling, which incensed me even more.

"Watson, resiliency — the ability to recover — is a sign of greatness." Then his humor was replaced with regret. "In their rush to close the case, they'll let some of the fish slip the net."

This caught me aback and my expression must have indicated it.

"Weems had to have contacts in the underworld. Not only to secure the stolen securities but to hire those bully boys that had a go at us."

"You have that Straithway chap in mind."

"Exactly. Unless Weems spills all, the ersatz so-licitor will probably remain at large. Well, it won't be the first time. They let Moriarty get away, as you recall."

The glow of Holmes' triumph had faded and I felt most discouraged about the whole matter.

13
The Revelations of Lady Teasdale

The following morning Holmes did not even show up for breakfast, and Mrs. Hudson clucked considerably at the manner in which I toyed with mine. I ignored the morning papers, sensing they would but serve as a reminder of an unwelcome memory.

To say that I was dissatisfied with the turn of events is an understatement. Holmes would be credited with the solution, for it was he alone who had contended that the appraiser's death had been contrived. The journals, having made much of the matter, would now hail it as another triumph for the finest mind in England. Brickstone would share in the bravos and solidify his position as police commissioner, having ostensibly backed my friend, but that did not nag at me. Somehow the case did not have that nice, tidy feeling about it.

It was late afternoon when Holmes finally favored me with his presence. As he sipped coffee, my efforts to excite further interest in the affair were not blessed with immediate success.

"Our loyalty in this matter lies with Claymore Frisbee, old chap. At his behest, we attempted to learn who had removed his friend from the land of the living. 'Tis done. The fact that Commissioner Brickstone has successfully ridden two horses to glory or that Frontnoy Leicester is desperately intent on keeping part of this case under wraps is of no matter."

"It doesn't feel right."

"Well said. I suspect that Brickstone, after conferring with the Prosecutor for the Crown, will agree with you." Holmes then took pity on my obvious confusion. "Good, old Watson. I fancy you pictured me confronting Weems with his actions as they did occur and, if I say so myself, his thoughts in the doing. Shocked by my revelation, the embezzler and murderer breaks down and confesses all."

"Well . . . yes," I admitted, "that did go through my mind."

"A possible oversimplification. If they find his cache of ill-gotten gains and establish how he sold Manheim's securities, it makes a pretty good case. Especially if they track down the underworld connections that supplied the stolen certificates. Not airtight, and there are some 'ifs'!"

"Suppose that you were still involved, Holmes. How would you nail that rascal, Weems, to the mast?"

"The girl is the key. Weems was not in desperate

straits. He had a good position with a leading firm in its field. However, Leicester is not going to step aside, and the organization might well collapse with his passing. Our university hero, turned account executive, was bored with his legal homelife and effected a liaison with this Vivian Sinclair. One primrose path leads to another, and his plan was to start anew elsewhere but start with ample funds to live the life he wished to become accustomed to."

"With Vivian Sinclair?"

"I would think so." Holmes opened a desk drawer, extracting the picture that Wallingford had secured.

"Have another look at her and see if you are in agreement. To me, she has a knowing air. A graduate of the university of the universe."

"You feel she is involved in the embezzlement, Holmes?" I asked as I surveyed the redheaded lady again. Not a painful task, I might add.

"If Weems planned to spirit her out of the country, she must know something."

Suddenly Holmes cocked his head to one side.

"It's Billy," he stated, "and not alone. The boys are with him."

The man's hearing was really abnormal, along with his ability to detect a familiar footfall. There was that gentle knock on the door, and our page boy opened it to admit Wallingford and Gilligan.

"Do be seated, gentlemen," said Holmes, as I made for the spirit cabinet. "I have a bit of news."

"So do we, Gov," stated Gilligan, nodding in my

direction. Without prompting, Billy departed for cold stout and some ice. Wallingford had become acclimated to England as a second country, but habits are another thing. Like his Yankee brethren, his libations were iced.

"It's on the street, Mr. Holmes," stated the American, "or it soon will be. On a hunch, I struck up an acquaintance with that Beacon reporter, Blatt. According to him, the Yard is after Weems, but so far, no luck. I picked up Slim and dropped in figuring there might be something doing."

"On the off chance, you know?" Gilligan sounded hopeful.

To cover his irritation at the news, Holmes crossed to the mantle, staring for a moment into the flames of the hearth fire.

"The cumbersome, official machine seems unable to assume motion without loud noises. This sounds like our old friend Lestrade's heavy-handed approach."

"What did Scotland Yard do?" I asked. "Send Weems advance notice?"

"Dunno, Doc," was Slim's response, "but that boy has dug himself in somewheres."

"Anything from Styles?" Holmes' question was delivered in an offhanded manner, but I was not fooled. He was still interested despite his apparent disassociation.

"Weems hasn't shown up at Vivian Sinclair's place, Gov."

"That is strange. On the run I would think, that

would be his first move."

"What's our move?" asked Wallingford. "My guess was Andrews, but Slim and I figured you had proved to the Commissioner that it was Weems. . . ."

"Exactly what happened," I interjected. "Then Brickstone took over the matter."

"He may live to regret it," was the American's sage comment.

"As for moves," said Holmes, "we're off the case."

"Gov, the peelers will blow it. We're not gonna let that 'appen, are we?" Gilligan actually sounded agitated.

"You see, Holmes, you can't drop it now," I exclaimed, taking advantage of the support provided by the lads.

"You, Watson, are the one who always chides me about those unimportant but frequently fascinating little puzzles we get involved in because they are unrewarding as well."

I played my trump card. "You swayed me when you stated that it was not the gain but the game."

Holmes looked towards Gilligan and Wallingford with resignation.

"Under reasonable circumstances, I am capable of bringing the most wily opponent to heel, yet I can't evade my oldest and dearest friend."

"Good show, Doc." As Slim congratulated me, Wallingford nodded his approval.

"So," said the sleuth, "again the game is afoot."

It would seem that fate heeded this statement for our loyal page boy was at the door, not with cold stout and ice, however.

"Lady Teasdale, ter see you, Sir, if you are 'avin' visitors?"

Four pairs of eyes exchanged inquisitive looks.

"Dear me," said Holmes, adjusting the collar of his purple dressing gown, "what could have prompted this visit?"

Then her ladyship was upon us. My patient swept into the room and was quite delighted to have four members of the opposite sex dancing attendance on her.

After greetings, she got to the matter upon her mind, never being the one to walk around a subject. At least that was my impression at the time.

"After our little escapade of last week, Mr. Holmes, I've been on tenterhooks, and now it is said that good looking Mr. Weems is a wanted man. Is he truly the culprit?"

"That is correct, Lady Teasdale," said Holmes.

"The little escapade," I added, "in which you were so helpful, turned out to be most important to Holmes' solution."

Her ladyship almost cooed and then her eye fell on the picture of Vivian Sinclair which was lying on our desk. "Well," she stated, "I trust this woman wasn't . . ."

Her ladyship had picked up the picture and now regarded it from another angle. "Hummm, that wig wouldn't fool anyone."

"Wig?" asked Holmes quickly.

"That red hair doesn't belong to her. Any woman would tell you that. I do believe I know her." Lady Teasdale rummaged in her purse for a moment, then secured her lorgnette and, with the aid of it, surveyed the picture critically.

"I do indeed — that's Gaye Farraday, and why would she be wearing a wig when she has quite lovely blond hair?"

"Gaye Farraday?" exclaimed Wallingford. There was something in the tone of his voice that caused me to regard him closely.

"You know her?" queried Holmes.

"The picture had me fooled until her ladyship identified her. Gaye Farraday is married to Holbrook D'Arcy whom I knew of in America." Wallingford's next words were directed to Lady Teasdale. "D'Arcy is what is known in my country as a confidence man, a highly reprehensible occupation."

Well, I thought, here is the kettle calling the pot black. D'Arcy, whom I had never heard of, may have been big in his field, but I'd wager he was never in the class of my friend, Wallingford.

"You mean," exclaimed Lady Teasdale, "that Gaye is married to an American criminal?"

"Actually, he's British but found it more expedient to operate his flim-flam on the other side."

During these revelations, Holmes had been pacing the room, his thin, aquiline face seemingly engaged in a study of the ceiling. There was an expression of distaste on his hawk-like features.

"Mark me for a fool on this one, Watson. I told you the girl was the key to finding Weems, but I didn't carry that thought far enough."

Holmes came to a halt to regard our titled visitor with that courtly charm that he exhibited to members of the opposite sex, even though he distrusted the effect they could have on rational thinking.

"Lady Teasdale, again we find ourselves in your debt. You asked about Geoffrey Weems and naught has changed. He did murder the appraiser, Wyndhaven, just as though he had fired a lethal bullet. He also is an embezzler. It would seem that is but the tip of the iceburg. The matter now plunges into far deeper waters, a complication which I had not foreseen but do now because of your timely information."

Her ladyship gave evidence of being quite overwhelmed by Holmes' gratitude, but I sensed there was something else going on in her mind. I had been her doctor for a long time.

" . . . and you are really too kind, Mr. Holmes." This concluded her modest disclaimers and now she got down to business. The matter of the murdered appraiser not being the real reason for her presence.

"There is a situation which has me sorely distressed, Mr. Holmes."

"If there is any way that I can assist . . .?" Holmes' expressive hands terminated his words with an expansive gesture, inviting disclosure.

My heart sank. In the parlance of the world of

pugilism, Holmes' statement would be referred to as "leading with your chin," for I well knew the importance that really minor matters can assume in the female mind.

"It is the question of my ball, Mr. Holmes. I planned the event for next Thursday. It's rather in memory of my dear, departed Basil, you see. Then that cat, the Duchess of Paisley and her crony, Lady Windermere, scheduled their Winter Ball at the Crystal Palace on the very same night. Historically, their affair opens the winter social season of London, you see, and there will be no one of importance at my party at all."

"Ah hah," I thought, "the kitten was caught at the cream." My patient had planned to slip in her social gathering in advance of the Duchess', but the Paisley-Windermere forces had rallied and dealt her a crushing blow. The first salvos of the eternal social wars of London during the winter season had already been fired. This fierce conflict of titled women-folk had never been of interest to Holmes, and I shuddered at the thought of what might be his response. He had made a sweeping offer, as befits an English gentleman under the circumstances, but Lady Teasdale's problem was akin to a client coming to him with a tale of marital strife.

Her ladyship was wily and some of my thoughts had already occurred to her.

"My little problems are hardly in your line, Mr. Holmes," she concluded, "but you are known as the finest mind in England, and I have hopes that you may come up with an idea."

"Well," I thought, "here we go."

If Holmes had ever surprised, nay dumbfounded me, this was the time. He was gazing thoughtfully into the hearthfire, and I noted Wallingford and Gilligan exchanging nervous looks for, to them, her ladyship's plea was tantamount to blasphemy. Then that noble head turned and the lips twitched at their ends, to me a signal that the eccentric genius was pleased.

"We take care of our own. Don't know who said that, but it's a good thought." The sleuth's lips had now curved into a genuine smile. "Besides, if the greatest mind in England can't come up with a solution to your difficulty, your ladyship, it had best abdicate that overgrandized position."

A wave of relief swept through our sitting room.

"The easiest solution or the first one would be a calling in of some old debts, but first, background is needed. I assume your invitations have been extended for some time?"

"Yes, Mr. Holmes, but few responses since the Duchess . . ."

"No mind. In planning an evening of this kind, there are certain acceptances that are vital? Certain personages who must be there to ensure the success of the affair?"

"Very true, Mr. Holmes."

"Then we must have a reason for your re-contacting the important guests, those who come to be seen and not to see. What more reasonable than an assurance that they can wear their finest gems without fear, despite the rash of recent jewel robberies?"

"What jewel robberies?" asked her ladyship.

"Mmmm, a point. Just mention that there has been a number on the continent, but your guests can feel secure since the Commissioner of New Scotland Yard, Cecil Brickstone, will be present, along with Mr. Sherlock Holmes."

"How clever."

"I would delay these second contacts since I'm in hopes that you can also announce, among your honored guests, the presence of Lord Bellinger, the Prime Minister, along with Lord Cantlemere and Baron Holdernesse."

My imperious patient seemed on the verge of apoplexy at the thought of the riches dropped into her lap. "The Prime Minister . . . Lord Cantlemere . . . why Mr. Holmes, no one will go to the Paisley affair at all."

Holmes shrugged. "Unfortunate, but then the Duchess never joined forces with a detective, did she?"

"I don't know what to say."

"When in doubt, say nothing," advised the sleuth. "By the way, your ladyship, how was it that your path crossed that of Gaye Farraday, also known as Vivian Sinclair, also Mrs. Holbrook D'Arcy?"

"Ah hah," I thought, "Holmes has thrown the weight of his power and prestige behind my patient, but there is a little something that he wants."

His question seemed to have struck a nerve, since

Lady Teasdale colored and glanced at the male faces in the room in embarrassment. Then she settled on me.

"Well, I do have my doctor here. Can I be assured that what I say will be held in confidence by the rest?"

Had Holmes not responded immediately, I would have.

"Your ladyship, you not only have your own doctor but, it would seem, your own private detective and associates. Your words will not leave this room."

"Well, gentlemen, when I met Sir Basil, I was a Gaiety Girl. I was a showgirl in the 'London Gaieties' at the Garrick.* I was not a performer in the true sense, for we show girls . . . well, our producer Flo had a wonderful taste in women's clothes. He had us gussied up like *le dernier cri,* you know. We would parade down a flight of stairs with a follow spot . . . spotlight that is . . . and that was about all there was to it. Flo spent money like water and we

---

*Ed. Note: The Garrick Theatre opened in 1889 and many references by Watson place this adventure as some time after that. Lady Teasdale refers to her producer as "Flo," not a common nickname. Could it be that Florenz Ziegfeld was trying out, in England, the formula he used so effectively in his world famous Ziegfeld Follies on the American musical stage? Ziegfeld was born in 1869 and died at the age of 63 in 1932, so he could have been in London at the time her ladyship refers to, and his nickname was "Flo." But I shall leave this for theatrical historians to puzzle out. It is interesting that Lady Teasdale mentions her "Flo" as spending lavishly. When Ziegfeld died, and he had had in one season four smash hits on Broadway at the same time, he was in debt to the tune of one million dollars, an unbelievable sum at that time. An amount to be reckoned with in our times as well.

really did look rather splendid. Little Gaye Farraday joined the Gaieties when she was very young. She lied about her age and everybody knew it, but she had a wonderful figure which was all Flo cared about. Underneath the show title, 'London Gaieties,' he had a motto, 'Dedicated to the Glorification of the British Beauty.'**

"It was that year that Sir Basil, who was a dashing figure in those days, used to wait for me at the Garrick alleyway every night with flowers or perfume or some wonderful gift."

"A regular Stage Door Johnny," commented Wallingford.

"I beg your pardon?" inquired her ladyship.

"An American expression. Means a chap who waits at the stage door for the love of his life."

"Well, that's a good description of dear Basil. He quite swept me off my feet, so I left the Gaieties to marry him. I later heard that Gaye had married some fellow in London and gone to America, but I rather lost track of my fellow Gaiety Girls."

Her ladyship paused and took a deep breath. I sensed that there was another tale untold, which proved to be the case.

"Shall we put it as it actually was, gentlemen? I did not just lose track of old friends. It was intentional on my part. If it ever is bruted about that I was a show girl, I wouldn't be able to hold up my head in society."

**The Follies glorified the American girl.

"We understand, Lady Teasdale," said Holmes gently. "I will be in touch with you shortly and perhaps we can put our minds, with Wallingford's assistance, to those follow-up messages you are going to send relative to your festivity. In the meantime, it is up to me to make good on certain promises and I will, rest assured."

I escorted my patient downstairs to her waiting carriage.

"Depend on Holmes, Lady Teasdale."

"Oh I shall . . . I shall, Doctor. He is quite a wondrous man."

"There's a little rhyme in the streets of London about him, you know.

> 'Holmes had but to reach out his hand
>   to touch the highest in the land.' "

It was a greatly reassured Lady Teasdale who left our lodgings.

Back in the sitting room, I found my fellow conspirators awaiting my arrival.

"Ah, Watson, now we can get to it, for your medical practice did us a good turn on this day."

"I must say, Holmes, your enormous and sudden enthusiasm does rather surprise me."

"As regards her ladyship? Well, we have a peculiar schism here between our titled gentry and our American cousins. The 'rags to riches' theme is much thought of in the colonies, whereas we seem to frown down upon it. I'm rather partial to the American approach myself. As regards the Wyndhaven tragedy, it was you and your cohorts here who wished to continue with the matter."

"Well, it has not been brought to a conclusion," I replied, somewhat lamely. I was gratified to see Wallingford and Gilligan nod in agreement.

"Decidedly not, because I was wrong."

Had I a tuppence for every time I heard Holmes say that, I would not have bus fare to Stoke Newington.

"The paint ran thin," continued the sleuth, "on one portion of my picture of what happened. Weems improvised his 'Masquerade Murder,'* that's true enough, and he was the instrument in an embezzlement plot, but the man had no previous record of criminal activities. The Yard came up with nothing, nor did the boys." Holmes indicated Wallingford and Gilligan. "Now, as you might say Watson, 'tis as plain as a pickstaff. Weems was not a natural criminal. This whole muddle we've been involved in is more in your line, Wally."

"Mine?" inquired a startled Wallingford.

"It has been a scam, a flim-flammery from the beginning. This D'Arcy fellow. . . ." Holmes had been pacing again but stopped to regard Wallingford.

"Do you happen to know him?"

"Not really. Never met him to my knowledge."

"But he knows you?"

"Well, certainly of me." Wallingford seemed

---

*Author's Note: That was the second time Holmes had used that descriptive phrase, which prompted me to select it as the title of this adventure. J.H.W.

slightly wounded by the thought that anyone in the confidence game would not be familiar with "Get Rich Quick" Wallingford.

"D'Arcy wouldn't happen to be tall with gray hair and a very pale complexion, would he?"

"That sounds like the bird," agreed our American associate.

For a brief instant, Holmes' eyes and mine exchanged an understanding look. The bogus solicitor, Straithway, was now identified. Unknowingly, we had the kingpin of this adventure in our hands briefly, but much water had flowed under the bridge since then.

The sleuth nodded with satisfaction. "It was D'Arcy, with access to stolen stocks and bonds, who selected Weems as the . . . er . . . 'mark' is the word, I believe."

"Right on, Mr. Holmes," responded Wallingford. "It fits, you know. As I recall, D'Arcy ran with a rough bunch."

"It's all coming together," said the sleuth, rather savoring his words. "I told Brickstone and Leicester that Weems had improvised a murder using the means at his disposal. That is exactly what we are going to do, gentlemen. We are going to plan a 'scam' using our assets at hand to catch this elusive Mr. D'Arcy. He had Vivian or Gaye or whatever we wish to call her get close to Weems, after which the broker was maneuvered into a criminal activity. As to our means. First, only we know about the woman, D'Arcy's wife. Slim, I want more men watching her."

Gilligan stroked his long jaw. "Well, Swifty Summers is in town and surely Styles can dig up a couple of good boys."

"Capital. All must be informed that the lady in question might try and make a run for it as a blond, not a redhead."

"I'll get on it first thing, Mr. 'Olmes."

"Good. Now Wally, we'll want a suite adjacent to the one occupied by Mrs. D'Arcy at that hotel. . . ."

"The Cartright," I exclaimed.

Holmes cast an approving look my way before continuing.

"In a pinch we could use the rooms above hers. Do what you can."

Wallingford nodded and the sleuth's eyes shifted back towards Gilligan.

"What is the latest on the lady? What does she do with herself?"

"Eats in the hotel, mostly. Goes to one of them new beauty salons."

"Beauty salons. Now there is a possibility. Check with Slippery and see when she last went to the beauty salon. It would be helpful to know if she has another appointment soon."

Slim grinned. "I figgers a place like that has to have an appointment book Gov, so maybe tonight somebody gets in there and takes a peek."

"Very good." The sleuth was rubbing his hands together and obviously having the time of his life with this "scam" of his, whatever it might be. "Now

Lady Teasdale's ball can certainly serve a purpose."

Gilligan had a thought. "About that there affair, Gov. You did mention some real heavyweight names as honored guests. Can we deliver?"

"The Prime Minister and Lord Cantlemere have good cause to do us a favor if it seems within their power. Even if it does not.* I doubt if the Duke of Holdernesse has forgotten so soon that it was Watson and I who found his kidnapped son, Lord Saltire."**

Slim was convinced. "I follow the drift, Gov."

"Brickstone will be no problem for I shall just promise the Commissioner a solution. By the time of Lady Teasdale's ball, he will be just as puzzled as he is right now."

"You don't think Scotland Yard will catch Weems?" I asked.

"No."

"Gov, they've got everybody available on the job. There's so many peelers in Limehouse and Soho I've a feelin' they may start arresting each other."

"And," added Wallingford, "there's descriptions of Weems from Edinburgh to Lands End."

"No doubt," responded Holmes calmly. "However, they are looking in the wrong places. That will be Watson's and my opening move. A discussion with Athelney Jones. You, Slim, take care of the Slippery Styles matter. Also, I want a rumor spread that the

---

*The Adventure of the Second Stain. The Adventure of the Mazarin Stone.
**The Adventure of the Priory School.

French 'Deuxieme Sept' gang of jewel thieves are here in London."

"But Holmes," I argued, "you caught them all."

The sleuth waved one hand in an aimless gesture as though to dismiss my objection.

"No matter, Watson. Perhaps they have been pardoned? Who is to know? I just want the expectation that something will happen at her ladyship's ball. Something will, of course, but not the expected. We might call it 'The Surprise Ball.' " Holmes swiveled towards the former confidence king. "Wally, I've a need of that devious mind of yours in planning this flim-flammery."

"Mr. Holmes," stated the American frankly, "I haven't the faintest idea what you are figuring to do."

"You will, Wally, you will." Holmes was pacing again. "All right, let's have at it. Watson and I will handle the Weems matter, a very necessary adjunct to this affair. Keep in touch, for things promise to be lively and there is much to do. Our excursion into the field of the confidence game is now under way."

As Billy showed the lads out, Holmes penned some words on a sheet of foolscap which allowed me to try to interject some sanity into the proceedings.

"Holmes, who is going to pay for all of this?"

"I even have an idea regarding that," he responded.

Well, I had been dissatisfied with the case. I had bemoaned my inability to arouse interest in Holmes. It was my patient, Lady Teasdale, who had provided the clue that sparked the fire in my friend. If I now found myself involved in another of Holmes' wild schemes, who was there to blame but myself?

Holmes handed me the foolscap. "Have Billy take care of this, will you Watson?" he asked, heading for his bedchamber.

It was the same message to be cabled to three destinations. First, the Prime Minister. Then a reigning political figure of fifty years standing who was one of the most irascible chaps one could find, and finally the richest man in England. Yet it was that same terse style that Holmes always used in his cablegrams.

"Extremely important to me that you attend Teasdale ball. Invitation forthcoming. Holmes."

Sheer madness from anyone else, but I knew they would be there.

14

The Flim Flam

Our page boy was dispatched with the Bellinger, Cantlemere, Holdernesse cables, along with some instructions which I was not privy to. Things were following a familiar pattern. Holmes had, for the moment at least, planned the actions of what I choose to call the "inside group." Gilligan, Wallingford and Styles were all members and known to me, but there were others whom I catalogued as the outside group. These I did not know nor did I want to. They never came to Baker Street and many might well know Holmes by a different name. I did know that the sleuth kept five separate establishments in various parts of London where he had as many different identities. It would not be long before he departed from our bachelor quarters, possibly in one of his many disguises, to haunt the byways of the underworld making contact with shadowy individuals and securing information which only he could unearth. The outside group was a vital cog in the machinery that my friend had pieced together through the years and there was little of import that happened in the teeming metropolis of six million that Holmes was not aware of in short order.

But now he was seated, pipe in hand, by the window, and that great mind was placing parts of the puzzle together and testing the strength of his reasoning and the firmness of the theories he had evolved.

I might well have done my friend an injustice in referring to some of his schemes as wild, but I was always suspicious of his pawkish humor. Also, my vision was limited to one matter at a time, whereas Holmes, when he unleashed an all-out effort, viewed the complete picture. The resolutions that he strove for covered every facet of the matter he was involved in. Cases not completely resolved irritated him and he had brooded about "The Adventure of the Engineer's Thumb" for years.

My ruminations as to my friend's methods and intense mental concentration were both broken off by the arrival of Inspector Athelney Jones.

In spite of myself, my heart went out to our red-faced, overweight, sometime friend. Jones looked as contrite as I had ever seen him, and that is a considerable statement. Of course, he had kept in contact with his newspaper friends and, following the winds and tides of the moment, had been quoted in print as having decided that all the speculation over Wyndhaven's death was naught but a tempest in a teapot. This typical blunder was harshly underscored by Holmes' solving the matter right after the publication of Jones' new-found opinion. Cecil Brickstone must have used strong language in informing the man that a statement by a, quote, veteran inspector, end quote, that was promptly disproved, was detrimental to the image of Scotland Yard and the office of the commissioner as well.

Jones did have a remarkable ability to leapfrog his errors, conveniently forget them and, indeed, blithely barge ahead as though they had never happened; but Brickstone's censure was a matter which he could not ignore.

As a result, it was a woebegone policeman who entered our sitting room, hat in hand, in fear that he wouldn't even be asked to seat himself.

Experience must have bred a tolerance in Holmes which he did not practice with many others.

"Seat yourself, Jones, and try to erase that hangdog expression," said my friend, and he cocked his eye at me with a "why not?" look. I rose and made for the spirit cabinet which prompted no objection from the inspector. As I busied myself with gasogene, glass and bottle, Jones addressed the great detective hesitantly.

Got your message, Mr. Holmes . . ." he began, but a gesture silenced him.

"I have asked myself previously what was to be done about you, Jones, but you are still here as am I, and no great damage was done by your much circulated theory."

"Beggin' your pardon, Sir, that is but a half truth. No harm to you but I'm standing on shaky ground at the moment."

"I suspected as much, which is why I've decided to make you a hero."

Stunned, Jones momentarily ignored the drink I offered him and then grasped it with shaky hands.

"You're 'aving me on a bit, aren't you Mr. Holmes?"

"No, but I may be fooling myself. I'm in hopes, heaven knows why, that you can keep something to yourself for a change."

"I will, Mr. Holmes, honor bound. I'm leavin' the theories to you. Just tell me what to do."

The sleuth regarded Jones for a long moment, then shook his head quickly as though regretting his next move. "Hope springs eternal," he half muttered and then his cold, analytical manner reasserted itself.

"Don't take notes, Jones. With your luck you would leave them on Brickstone's desk. Now, the Yard is in desperate pursuit of Geoffrey Weems."

"They are, Sir. I mean, we are, indeed. The Commissioner seems quite beside himself."

"The prize snatched away becomes more desirable," said Holmes drily. "They are not going to find a live Weems, but you are going to find a dead one."

"You mean he's had it, Mr. Holmes? How do you know?"

"Because as a fugitive, Weems is a liability, for he is an amateur. Before exposure, he was unique for those who had selected him as a tool. He had position, reputation, entry to the Leicester files, everything needed for a quite ingenious swindle."

Jones was mopping his ruddy face with a limp handkerchief.

"I'm not tuned in to all of this, Mr. Holmes."

"There is no need. You are going to search, Jones, for a corpse of Weems' description. It will take some doing, but I want you to send inquiries to the station of every district with access to the water from say . . . Harwich to Margate. I'm betting the body has been disposed of in the Thames, though you might cover the Plumstead Marshes area as well. I'll also wager that you know a number of constables in the outskirt districts. Put them at the top of your list."

"Mr. Holmes, you've handed me a handful."

"Jones," said Holmes, leaning forward in his chair and staring into the inspector's small, deepset eyes; "hero!"

"Hero?" echoed Jones, who then tapped his chest with an index finger. "Me?"

"Exactly."

"Hero," repeated Jones, savoring the word as though he had discovered a new and irresistible flavor.

The inspector's momentary daydream was interrupted by the familiar soft tattoo on our door and then Billy was with us.

"It's Commissioner Brickstone and that Mr. Leicester to see you, Mr. 'Olmes," he announced.

The sleuth was on his feet in an instant, a long and sinewy arm dragging Jones erect as well.

"Billy," commanded the sleuth, "you are to take

Inspector Jones down the back way to the yard gate. I will handle our visitors."

Urging a befuddled inspector towards the rear, Holmes' words came with the speed of bullets. "Jones, if you find what I think you will, contact me before you report to Brickstone."

As our page boy and the inspector headed for the back stairs, Holmes crossed to our front door and the landing beyond.

"Ah, Commissioner," he called down, "do come up, will you? Your . . . er . . . companion as well, of course."

Re-entering our chambers, Holmes gestured towards the end table adjacent to our visitor's chair.

"Quick, Watson, dispose of that glass," he whispered. "Our conference with Jones is best a secret for the while."

I hastened to grab Jones' half finished drink and had it concealed in the spirit cabinet and myself in the vicinity of the couch when Brickstone and Leicester entered the room.

Whereas Jones had been contrite, the commissioner was trying, unsuccessfully, to suppress a sheepish expression. Frontnoy Leicester, in his wake, was grim of face and tense in manner. Greetings were stiff and formal and my offer of liquid refreshment was refused. The commissioner did accept a cigar, however, though Leicester did not.

Seated and ill at ease, our visitors exchanged a glance as though undecided as to who would make the first move. It was Brickstone who opened the proceedings.

"Look here, Holmes, we seem to be in a bit of a spot."

"Geoffrey Weems being particularly elusive, I gather," commented the sleuth. His manner towards Cecil Brickstone was cordial enough, but he took no pains to conceal a distinct coldness towards Frontnoy Leicester. Holmes, unless his reputation and abilities were questioned, did not make a practice of displaying hostility or any other feelings, for that matter. It came to my mind that he was adopting the role of the affronted and rejected talent in no mood to let bygones be bygones.

"We can't find him," admitted Brickstone, "and that's a fact. It would seem that your thoughts regarding a more cautious approach to the matter were justified. We're looking at an empty sack, for we have neither the murderer nor the money he embezzled."

There was a silence which Holmes broke after a moment.

"By 'we' do you mean you, Commissioner, and Mr. Leicester?" he asked.

"Well, there are these complications . . ." began Brickstone.

"Dash it all," exploded Frontnoy Leicester, "can't you see he's way ahead of us?" The aged financier then addressed himself to Holmes, his tone reeking of defiance.

"I was the odd man in this affair. I desperately wished to keep the Manheim matter under wraps, for it is the end of me if it gets out. I hoped, with Weems in our grasp, that we could make some sort of deal and present a different motive for his crime. Delusions, dreams, lunacy, call it what you will, but I had no thought of misdirecting justice, believe me in that."

Holmes nodded, preserving his silence.

"Nor did I," interjected Brickstone hastily. "There is the matter of public confidence, however, which gives appeal to some sort of adjustment. . . ."

Since the commissioner was wandering in a verbal circle, Leicester retrieved the conversational ball. "Naturally, all of Manheim's securities will be replaced out of my pocket. I've already begun that operation." The thought made the financier wince. "But with Weems at large and the notoriety that's attached itself to the search for him, there will be doubt and confusion in the public mind. I'm feeling the effects, businesswise, already."

Holmes posed a question. "As an outsider, may I inquire as to your next move?"

"Being here," replied Brickstone, "is our next move. You were investigating this matter before my men were seriously involved. You could know or suspect or surmise something that might untangle this ball of yarn."

Holmes had a point to make and he was not subtle in the making.

"I had a client in this case whose wishes have been satisfied. Now . . ." He shrugged and let the conversation dangle there.

Leicester seized upon this statement, and there was the look of the horsetrader in his eyes.

"Since you are free to make other arrangements, would you take on this case in my behalf?" he asked.

"To find Weems and to try and keep his pillaging of the Manheim securities a secret if possible?"

"Yes. Yes," agreed Leicester eagerly. "There is the matter of your fee, of course."

"There is indeed," replied Holmes; and I was proud of him when he stopped right there. My friend shared the reluctance of his fellow countrymen to discuss financial matters. The tremendous amounts which he received in certain cases were offers, not the results of bargaining. In this matter, he was not displaying any reluctance to adopting a distinctly hard-nosed attitude.

"What amount would you consider sufficient?" asked Leicester cautiously.

"I will make the same arrangements as with my last client. A fee of my choosing."

Leicester was in a desperate position, but the methods of a lifetime are not easily put aside. Alarm ran roughshod over his face.

"Good heavens, that's tantamount to signing a check and leaving the filling out to you."

"It certainly is." The aged financier got no argument there.

It was with difficulty that Leicester brought his feelings under control.

"All right, Mr. Holmes. You shall have your pound of flesh. Just resolve this matter in the manner we agreed." Then animosity forced him to continue. "If you can, that is."

Holmes' nostrils flared, but he was not one to bury the hatchet too deep. It took him but a brief moment and then he was again the calm theorist of Baker Street.

He rose from his chair by the hearth, an obvious signal that the discussion was terminated.

"All right, gentlemen, I will devote my energies to the matter." His eyes found Brickstone's. "While you continue your investigation."

"Definitely," agreed the commissioner. Frontnoy Leicester was in haste to remove himself from surroundings that had caused him embarrassment. He was out the door and headed down the stairs before Brickstone had gathered himself together.

"The old boy's put out. Can't say I blame him. That knighthood that was rumored around may continue to be just a rumor." A trained politician, the commissioner made a point of shaking hands with both Holmes and myself before departing.

I wanted to congratulate Holmes on his financial negotiations, but suppressed this idea. Rather at a loss, I referred to the search the sleuth had instigated.

"You certainly fired up Jones."

"Actually, our inept friend is well suited for the job. He's put in the years and, because water seeks its own level, I picture many of his cronies of the past being shuttled off to backwater divisions, the very areas we are interested in. Now I must. . . ."

"A moment, if you will." I couldn't let Holmes off the hook yet. "What if Jones fails?"

"We are staking much on a single throw of the dice," admitted my friend. "In making that decision, I put myself in D'Arcy's place, asking myself what I would do in the situation that has developed. I just hope I haven't overestimated the man."

"I thought the danger was in underestimating one's opponent?"

"D'Arcy is not behind bars so I credit him with some intelligence. If logical, he will follow the path that I've charted. It is the only way for him to go. However, if he is but a bungler who fell into a fortunate situation, then it is we who shall be gazing at an empty sack, to quote the Commissioner."

"Forgive my density Holmes, but why your conviction that Weems is dead?"

"Alive, he represents the only way of tying our Mr. D'Arcy into the matter. We know, because of certain information we chanced upon, that D'Arcy is the real villain but we haven't a shred of evidence. As for Brickstone and his boys, they don't even know D'Arcy exists."

As was so often the case, Holmes' sensible answer had but deepened my mystification.

"If Weems is dead . . . ?"

"I think his removal was planned from the beginning. It was but a matter of time."

"All right, but with him unable to testify, how do we get to D'Arcy?"

Of a sudden, my friend's lips twitched into a tight

half smile that imparted a chilling expression to his face.

"If necessary, we shall create the connection, the thing that ties friend D'Arcy to the embezzlement and the murder of his co-conspirator."

That was all I could get from Holmes, for he had other things on his mind. I heard him rummaging around in his sleeping quarters and then he summoned Mrs. Hudson to inquire about a certain baggy parasol which was informative. Holmes was on the move and would be leaving Baker Street in his old woman disguise, one of his finest creations.

A precept of my dear, departed mother was "One thing at a time." This philosophy was of scant use to me now. It was as though the orchestra called "destiny" had segued from a largo movement into a fast march. It was my duty to remain on the premises as a connective link between the forces that Holmes had set in motion, but I did not lack for company, nor for news either. Wallingford was the first to report in and stated that he had rented the suite next to Vivian Sinclair at the Cartright Hotel which, fortunately, was available. Given the time, I had Wally demonstrate to me, in detail, something that he had but told me about previously.

"It's the oldest con in the book, Doc. The envelope switch and, you know, you've got it down pretty good."

"Thanks to you," I said, gratefully. "It would suit my purposes if my new found talent remained our secret."

"Sure thing. Boy, what I could have done with you in the old days. You'd have made a great bunko artist."

"I would?" I trusted the spirit of my dear mother was not privy to this fact.

"You've got an honest-looking face."

Next Holmes reappeared, not in the same garb in which he had departed, so I knew he had changed identities somewhere along the way. From his expression, I deduced that his foray into dark corners had not been revealing.

He admitted as much. "Not one of the contacts I could reach even knows of D'Arcy."

"Understandable, Mr. Holmes," was Wally's thought. "He probably made a fat score in the States and felt a trans-Atlantic journey would be good insurance. If he is 'hot' back home, it figures that he would lay low over here."

Darkness had fallen when Gilligan appeared, and there was that sly look about him that made me suspect his news was good.

"Vivian Sinclair is booked to have her hair washed and coiffed, whatever that is, at one in the afternoon tomorrow," he stated with satisfaction.

This somewhat unusual announcement seemed to please Holmes immensely.

"Things are falling together. Let us hope that our good fortune continues. Now, here's the way we work it. Wally has secured the suite next to the Sinclair woman, and I want you, Slim, in it when she leaves for the beauty salon tomorrow. While she's there, you get into her apartment and fashion a listening post. A hole behind a picture could do it. I want to be able to overhear whatever occurs in her apartment. We'll have someone there around the clock."

"Consider it done, Gov."

The sleuth now centered on our American ally.

"Wally, I want you to contact Lady Teasdale. I would like her ladyship at that beauty salon tomorrow when Mrs. D'Arcy arrives. She's to recognize her old showbusiness friend and, in the course of reminiscing, invite her to the ball." Holmes regarded me quizzically. "Do you feel she might need persuasion to undertake another charade for us, Watson?"

"I think she'll jump at the chance to play detective again," was my prompt response.

Now everything was coming into focus. My patient's social extravaganza was the lure. The former Gaye Farraday would wish to go as would so many other women at this moment.

"The invitation to Mrs. D'Arcy being 'with escort' ? " I asked.

"Exactly," responded Holmes. "We can't locate D'Arcy, so his wife will bring him to us. They must have some line of communication in case of a crisis. The woman will send her husband a message. He will show up at her rooms and now you know why I wanted extra manpower. When D'Arcy leaves, I want four men trailing him. Two on foot and two in a carriage. We'll find his rat hole and, when he leaves it to go to Lady Teasdale's affair, we'll pay it a visit."

"The money," exclaimed Wally. "The money Weems embezzled . . . you think we'll find it?"

"I think it is in his hideout," said Holmes. "D'Arcy has kept undercover, steering clear of his wife in case anyone knew about her connection with Weems. When everything seems safe, they are to join forces again and depart for new pastures. At least that is their plan."

Holmes had taken the ingredients at his disposal and baked a fancy cake indeed. But first, there was the matter of the missing Weems to be dealt with.

15

Watson in Charge

The problem of the fugitive embezzler and murderer came to a head much sooner than I had expected. It was my feeling that Holmes had patterned a series of incidents that had to come off on schedule or the culmination would fall apart. He had been fooled in assuming that Weems was the sole villain of the drama. As if in retaliation for being in error, he was determined to use those factors that investigation and fate had placed at our disposal along with the special aptitudes of the chessmen of his color that were maneuvering on the board. But what good his baited trap for Holbrook D'Arcy without Weems, alive or dead? If the account executive were not found, no connection 'twixt the purloining of the securities in the Manheim file and D'Arcy could be established, or so it seemed to me. To compound this difficulty, the master sleuth had selected the bumbling Athelney Jones to track Weems down. If that was not putting faith in a frail reed, I would like to know what was.

My estimation of the situation proved wrong, certainly nothing unusual. It was almost as though the march of events was preordained to follow the beat of Holmes' drummer simply because the great sleuth had planned it that way. My long association with that unique man had bred some strange ideas in my mind. As an instance, I had the eerie conviction that great steam engines propelling crack trains of England and the Continent were aware of the presence of the world's greatest detective, and their pistons and wheels followed Holmes' timetable rather than the one devised by a dispatcher. In truth, if all of the vague and mystical semi-ideas I entertained regarding Holmes were printed and made public, attendants from a mental institution would be on my trail and my mail would be forwarded to a padded cell.

The sleuth and I were in the middle of breakfast when Billy appeared, a cable on his silver tray. Our cockney page boy was no fool regarding "the investigation business," which he took most seriously.

"I got the messenger standin' by below, Mr. 'Olmes, just in case."

Holmes had eagerly torn open the envelope, and his intense eyes were devouring the words it contained.

"Capital thought, Billy. Return message as follows: 'Stand by — let no one touch weapon or body till my arrival with authorization.' Have you got it?"

"Right on, Mr. 'Olmes." Alerted by the sleuth's manner that time was of the essence, Billy made fast tracks to the hallway below.

Already Holmes was into his suit coat and reaching for his overcoat and hat.

"Come, Watson. We must hasten to the Commissioner's office before some hidebound official makes the error of destroying vital clues."

I was reaching for my bowler hat when an idea struck.

"I'll call to Billy and have him locate a carriage."

"No need, old chap. Phineas Portney has been on standby below since the early morning hours."

The page boy must have signalled our picturesque driver, for Phineas had the carriage door open as we dashed through the ground floor door.

"Mornin' Sir . . . Doctor. . . ."

"The Yard, Portney. Brickstone's office and let's hope that Susie is well-rested."

The spavined mare had been regarding us with wise eyes that peered out from under her tattered straw bonnet and, when the carriage door slammed shut behind us and Phineas scrambled to his perch, we took off with a jerk. I do not contend that Holmes could talk to horses, but animals are sensitive to moods, and speed seemed the order of the day to Susie. We took the first turn off Baker Street on two wheels and Holmes and I had to secure handholds as the ancient four wheeler swayed alarmingly.

"The cablegram, Holmes . . . what . . .?"

"From Athelney Jones, as you must suspect. He found the body of Weems in the morgue of the station at Gravesend. Shot in the temple by a Smith-

Wesson .38 calibre revolver found in the corpse's right hand. I was wrong about the body being dropped in the Thames. No identification and the case is on the station books as suicide."

"My Lord," I gasped as we took another corner. "A fugitive with the whole weight of Scotland Yard searching for him; the chap must have cracked up."

"The deuce you say, Watson. Suicide we don't accept, for it does not fit into my plans. If the police at Gravesend have not pawed over the weapon and corpse, forensic medicine may come to our rescue and I have the very man in mind. Thank heavens for Hans Gross. His book was so well received that it gives us a lever to move those dunderheads at the Yard in the direction of modern scientific investigation."

Bracing myself against the abrupt movements of our carriage and, hoping that we would arrive at Scotland Yard in one piece, I managed a complaint that was certainly well-founded.

"Holmes, I haven't the slightest idea of what you are talking about."

"Forgive me, old chap, no reason that you should. All rather recent, you see. You do know that for years I've contended that criminal investigation is stultified by the aversion of the authorities towards scientific advancement. When we first met, do recall that I had just discovered a re-agent precipitated by hemoglobin and nothing else."

"A medico-legal discovery you called it. Well, it certainly made the old guaiacum test outdated."

"Yet, it took a long time before it was put into general use as a reliable test to identify blood. A short while back this Hans Gross published his *Handbuch fur Untersuchungsrichter,** in which he advocated a philosophy of drawing upon the expertise of scientists to aid investigators and supply proof for use in court. Perhaps because Gross was a magistrate rather than a scientist, his work had quite an impact, certainly more than my complaints through the years."

"Well, Holmes, you are referred to as the scientific detective. Perhaps your style will become more common in the future."

"I devoutly hope so and better sooner than later."

Holmes sent his card in to Brickstone and, almost immediately, we were admitted to the commissioner's office.

"Holmes," exclaimed Cecil Brickstone, "you've obviously heard the news, though I cannot figure out how."

"As you have mentioned, from time to time I have my sources," responded the sleuth evasively.

"As soon as Jones cabled me, I notified Frontnoy Leicester. If he doesn't have a stroke, I imagine he will be here shortly."

"The prospect of Weems committing suicide must have been a shock to him," commented Holmes drily.

"In what way?" I asked, looking from my friend

---

*Gross' book, considered a classic, was published in 1893.

to the commissioner in puzzlement.

"The embezzled money," replied Holmes.

Commissioner Brickstone was more explicit. "Legally, a suicide is considered temporarily insane. Who knows what an insane person might do with the proceeds of the sale of Manheim's securities?"

On the heels of this remark, Leicester arrived. The aged financier did look very distraught.

"My God, Brickstone," he almost shouted, "this is monstrous."

"Before we re-hash this latest incident, gentlemen, I am in a considerable hurry." Holmes' tone and manner silenced the others or perhaps they were just unable to get a word in edgewise.

"You," stated the sleuth, indicating Leicester with an outstretched finger, "are concerned about the embezzled money. Well, I don't think it is at the bottom of the Thames and I do think I can find it." Holmes swung around towards the Commissioner. "There's something I need and promptly. You have a young pathologist here, Bernard Spilsbury,* whom I've had my eye on for some time. Can you send him with me to Gravesend with authorization to inspect the body and the death weapon and, if necessary, have Spilsbury perform an autopsy?"

"Why . . . yes," stammered Brickstone.

"I would be most grateful if you would make the

---

*Holmes certainly picked his man here. Bernard Spilsbury, who became world famous because of the Crippen case in 1910, was destined to go down in history as the world's first great criminal pathologist. For over three decades, he dominated forensic medicine in England. In 1922 he was knighted by King George V.

arrangements. Oh, it would be well to notify those in charge down there to keep their hands off the Smith-Wesson and Weems' body as well."

"I'll cable Athelney Jones immediately. Being from the Yard, he is in charge."

As Holmes drew me to one side for instruction, Brickstone had to get in one question or risk a nervous breakdown.

"Holmes, I've had my best men in the field searching for this Weems fellow. How in the name of all that is holy did Jones, of all people, find him?"

"I would guess," replied the sleuth blandly, "that the Inspector figured everyone else was looking for a live Weems so he would search for a dead one."

The Commissioner accepted Holmes' fabrication promptly. "By Jove, I believe you've got it. That is just the kind of reasoning that blunderer would come up with."

Leicester had been trying to say something, but Brickstone ignored him, calling for his assistant. Holmes had words for my ears only, so the financier preserved his silence. It was that or talk to a wall.

"Watson," said my friend, *sotto voce,* "it's up to you to take command at Baker Street during my absence. If I am delayed, get over to the suite that Wally has taken at the Cartright Hotel. I'm of a mind that D'Arcy will show up after his wife contacts him, and I'm particularly interested in what they say to each other. Also in the boys tailing D'Arcy when he leaves."

"Slippery Styles and his lads will do the job,

Holmes."

"I'll feel better with you coordinating things."

I had never been so proud in my life and resolved that we would ferret out D'Arcy's hiding place if I had to do it myself.

16
The Second Murder

Back in our chambers on Baker Street, I notified Billy that all members of the working group were to be admitted immediately. Then I fell to wondering what Holmes expected to find in Gravesend and why he had wished to have one Bernard Spilsbury, whom I had never heard of, with him. There being no answers to these puzzles, I began to fret about the events scheduled for this afternoon and what report would reach me first. A sheer waste of time, of course, since Wallingford figured to be at the top of the list and he was. The light in his eyes had a soothing effect on my highly nervous condition.

"Her ladyship did us proud, Doc. She and the former Gaye Farraday fell all over each other when they just happened to meet." The American's right eyelid closed in a slow wink. "I was present, making an appointment for a fictitious woman, just in case Lady Teasdale needed a helping hand, which she didn't."

"Then D'Arcy's wife swallowed the invitation to

the ball bit?" I asked, on tenterhooks.

"Eagerly," was Wally's reassuring response. "Like a lot of chorus girls, former or otherwise, this toots reads the society pages, top to bottom. She knew all about Lady Teasdale's ball and the list of honored guests. In fact, she knew so much that she gave me a momentary scare."

"How was that?"

"She wanted to know if Sherlock Holmes would really be present. She was particularly interested in the boss and wondered if her ladyship knew him."

"We hadn't figured on that question."

"Didn't phase Lady Teasdale at all. She said that Mr. Holmes was quite close with the Commissioner of Police. One of those good answers that actually says nothing." Wally paused for a moment, thoughtfully. "You know, your patient has a natural feel for the con. If I hadn't mended my ways, I would take you and her ladyship back to the States and we could resell the Carpet Covered Carpet Tack Company all over again."

"Now wait a minute, Wally, you don't mean. . . ."

As my voice dwindled away, the American nodded. "Sure did, Doc, to a fellow in Akron, Ohio."

I felt that I was being joshed. "That's the most ridiculous sounding name for a company. . . ."

"That's the whole idea. That's also why the chap never pressed charges. He got to thinking what his friends at the country club would say when they learned what he had bought."

"But how did you sell it to him to begin with, this nonexistent company?"

Wally shook his head as though in wonderment at my naivete.

"Doc, it's not what you sell, it's how you do it."

With difficulty, I dragged my thoughts from the fascinating Carpet Covered Carpet Tack Company and back to business.

"You figure Slim had enough time for his job in the woman's apartment?"

Wally was confident. "Sure thing. I think he will use the hole-in-the-wall idea."

"If it is behind a picture, won't that muffle the sound of voices?"

"Shouldn't, too much. If there's any problem, we'll use the glass trick."

My blank stare must have been very obvious, and Wally took pity on me.

"You take a common drinking glass and put the top against the wall and your ear to the bottom. Sound is vibratory, isn't it?"

I had to admit to this.

"The open end of the glass catches the vibrations and relays them to your ear. There's some amplification, you see."

I didn't, but I was sure the man knew what he was talking about.

"Obviously, there are tricks to every trade," I conceded.

"For sure, Doc. If you ever want to take up safe-cracking, you've already got a great piece of equipment."

"What, pray tell, is that?"

"Your stethoscope. You put it against the safe, see, just like you're listening for a heartbeat. Only now you're listening for the tumblers."

"I'll leave that kind of work to Slim." Of a sudden, I realized that my nerves had settled down. "So," I thought to myself, "my eagle-eyed friend has been calming me." I knew some members of my profession who could not read a patient as well as Wallingford.

"How long before the next move?" I asked, rising to my feet and taking a turn around the room. I was reminded of Holmes when he was conjuring up an idea.

"Kinda depends on whether Mrs. D'Arcy goes back to her hotel or not. My guess is that she'll head for the nearest cable office."

"You think that's her line of communication with her husband?"

"The mail is too slow. There might not be a telephone where D'Arcy is holed up. I'm betting on a cable."

We had to wait for what seemed like ages to learn if Wally had won his bet. However, the ex-confidence man kept me diverted with tales of former days, so it really wasn't all that bad.

Finally a thin, quite dapper man of medium height with shiny black hair, entered our rooms. Wally made the introductions.

"This is Swifty Summers, Doctor. Gilligan's

friend. This here is Doctor Watson, Swifty."

"Pleased to meet you, Doc."

"What's the set-up as of now?" asked Wally.

"Gilligan is in your place at the hotel. Styles and the rest of the boys are positioned on the street, and I've got to hustle back. Slippery wanted Mr. Holmes to have this."

Very carefully, Summers took a piece of paper from his side pocket. It was a cable form from one of the pads made available for writing messages. He placed it gently on the desk.

"Slippery and I covered the D'Arcy woman from her hotel to the beauty salon, using the front and back tail. When she was finished there, she made a beeline for the Guilford Street cable office. I played Mr. Outside and Slippery went in behind her. She sent a cable but quick like. When she left I stayed with her, and Slippery managed to get this from the pad she wrote her message on. He figgers Mr. Holmes might be able to do something with it, being it's the underneath sheet and all."

"He will," I said, "for I know Holmes has been doing some experiments on that sort of thing lately." I was most happy to add to the general knowledge since, so far, the man who was supposed to coordinate matters had done absolutely nothing.

"Any message fer Slippery, Doctor?" asked the black-haired man.

"Errr . . . no. Mr. Holmes had to take a short trip. As soon as he returns, I fancy we will be there."

"There's time," stated Swifty. "The mark won't

pick up the cable on delivery. Ta-ta."

Swifty was, of a sudden, gone and I did not hear his footfalls on the stairs outside. Like Slippery Styles and Slim Gilligan, he was one of the silent type that appeared and disappeared genie-like.

"What did he mean by that last remark?" I asked Wally.

"All Swifty knows is that somebody's being set up for a tail job so, to him, D'Arcy is the mark."

"No, I meant about the cable."

"Well, Doc, his wife isn't going to wire D'Arcy direct, him hiding out you see. They've got some relay station worked out."

Despite my years with Holmes, there were still a great many things that I had to learn.

It was coming on towards night when Holmes finally appeared, and his familiar features were most welcome, for I was beginning to wonder if I should get over to the Cartright Hotel and the listening post without him.

Between us, Wally and I informed Holmes of our visit from the dapper Swifty Summers. The sleuth registered approval.

"Knowing Slippery, I imagine he treated this with care," he said, surveying the cable form.

"Summers handled it like it was going to explode," quipped Wally.

Carrying the form by its edges, Holmes made for his chemical corner and lit the gas jet under a retort which he half-filled with water.

"What did you learn at Gravesend?" I asked,

knowing that my friend, in the midst of his tubes and vials, would respond automatically, his mind on his work. This was a little trick that I had used before.

"Weems did not commit suicide. It was meant to look that way, but it was a sloppy attempt at deception. I scarce needed Bernard Spilsbury, but it was just as well that he was present since his findings confirmed mine and will be the official report."

Wally's eyebrows rose. "Spilsbury?"

"A young chap pioneering in forensics at the Yard. He realizes the importance of new methods even though there are many there who don't. He will make his fame or I am very much mistaken. Juries tend to view scientific investigations with distrust, but this will change." Holmes dropped some white crystals into a beaker which he placed under the neck of the retort. He then raised the flame under the vessel slightly.

Wally's face registered confusion, unusual for him. I gestured to him to remain silent.

"How did you know Weems . . . ?"

"Didn't kill himself?" interrupted Holmes in that detached voice that signified his concentration was elsewhere. "Fingerprints told the story, no need for an autopsy." The sleuth added a small amount of a brownish powder to the crystals in the beaker. The neck of the retort was beginning to emit steam.

"Silliest thing in the world, you know. Sir William James Herschel came up with the idea of fingerprints way back in 1857. Edwin Henry has been working on a method of classification. A murder was

solved and a conviction secured on the basis of a
thumbprint in far off La Plata, Argentina, in 1892.
Yet our authorities haven't adopted the usage of fingerprints yet."*

"About Weems," I said with a patience born of
practice.

"Oh, yes. He supposedly shot himself in the right
temple with a Smith-Wesson .38, yet there were no
powder marks on his face. There would have been
had he held the revolver to his head and fired. There
was a clear set of prints belonging to Weems on the
Smith-Wesson, but not another mark or smudge on
the gun. Obviously the weapon had been wiped
clean and then placed in the dead man's hand after
which Weems' fingers were closed around the butt
of the revolver."

Considerable steam had come out of the neck of
the retort and into the beaker by now. The sleuth
placed a cover over the beaker and turned off the gas
jet.

"If that wasn't enough, Weems' prints were absolutely clear and well-defined. If he'd actually shot
himself, the recoil of the Smith-Wesson would have
blurred his prints."

My friend picked up the beaker and shook it gently for a moment and then replaced it on the surface
of his chemical stand.

"Now let's see what message was sent to D'Arcy

---

*Holmes was quite indignant about this, all the more so since Scotland
Yard waited until 1901 before officially adopting fingerprints and the
Henry system of classification.

by his wife and cohort."

As Wally and I crossed towards him to observe, Holmes removed the cover from the beaker and placed the cable form on top of it. Faintly, I could detect vapor rising in the beaker. Then words imprinted on the form by the weight of penstrokes began to appear in a bluish color. Holmes read the message as it became more legible.

"Addressed to a Mr. D. Holbrook, care of general delivery, Prescott Street post office."

"The relay station you mentioned," I said to Wallingford.

"Important you come tonight. I'll be waiting. F.," continued Holmes, who then regarded Wally and myself. "No more than a confirmation of what we expected. Considering the hour, what say we hasten to the Cartright Hotel and hear what Mr. and Mrs. D'Arcy have to say to each other?"

17

The Great Tail Job

Phineas Portney and his dependable mare, Susie, got us to the hotel in jig time. On the way, Holmes had some cautionary advice.

"Slim has arranged a means of eavesdropping or we would have heard from him. Let us keep our words at a whisper level when inside Wally's rooms. If we can hear the D'Arcy woman and company, the reverse is true."

We entered the Cartright Hotel singly to avoid attracting attention and were soon gathered at the appointed place. It was Slim Gilligan who let us into the rooms. His first move was to point out a neat hole drilled into the east wall of the sitting room. Still in dumb show, he indicated that all was well. I placed my ear against the hole and could hear, quite clearly, sounds of movement and the opening and closing of several doors. Using my imagination, I pictured Mrs. D'Arcy alone, going through her wardrobe, a natural activity for a woman planning to attend a social function. When I was satisfied, Slim produced an added touch with the flourish of a prestidigitator. He had a cork which he placed in the hole.

"Now Gov, we can talk normal like." He gestured towards the cork. "I checked that out with one of the lads in here talking to himself. The plug does the job."

I was shaking my head in wonderment. "Slim, you think of everything."

As the cracksman grinned, Holmes had a suggestion. "You might complete that statement, Watson, by adding the words, 'in advance.' That's the key to the well-organized operation."

Taking Holmes and me to the large, curtained window, Slim drew the draperies slightly to one side, indicating where Slippery Styles and his crew were positioned and the carriage that they had standing by.

"If the bloke shows, our boys should be able to cover him like a tent when he leaves, Gov. I don't figure this D'Arcy for a green hand, and he must know a thing or two about coverin' his tracks, but Slippery's boys have been to the wars before. They're a good lot."

Holmes stepped back from the window signifying approval. "It is as well set up as it can be. Good job, Slim."

"Styles will be glad to hear that, fer the tail job is his department."

"When D'Arcy leaves, we'll know it. What's the signal to Slippery and his lads?" asked the sleuth.

"Wally here pulls the curtain aside and stands in

the window looking out," replied Gilligan. "Nothin'
suspicious, fer this is his apartment."

I had a sudden thought. "Let me get this straight.
D'Arcy leaves, we signal the boys on the street and
two follow him on foot."

"Styles and Lacy," said Slim.

"Two more are in a carriage tailing him as well,
right?"

"Swifty Summers and that Fenn fellow."

"The carriage they are using is standing by, supposedly empty. Let's say D'Arcy flags it."

"Swifty says he's waiting for a fare," explained
Gilligan.

"All right, but Portney is also on standby.
Wouldn't D'Arcy think it strange, two carriages
waiting for fares? This is a quiet neighborhood."

Holmes, who had been regarding me intently, let
a slow smile soften his aquiline features.

"You do channel one's thinking," he said.
"You've led me, unerringly, to a capital thought.
When the chap leaves we also signal Phineas and, if
D'Arcy wants a carriage, let's try and have him pick
Portney's. With the man in our own vehicle, the
trailing should be simplicity itself."

"Blimey, why didn't I think of that?" complained
Gilligan.

Holmes signalled for silence and opened the hole
in the wall to listen for a moment. Then he replaced
the cork.

"No sound so all's well. You prompted the idea,
Watson. Why not pop down and explain the matter

to Portney. Have him relay this new plan to Styles."

"Right away, Holmes," I said, feeling quite proud of myself.

Wally opened the door and, after a look down the hallway, I slipped out and made for the lifts. I was reaching for the button when one of two doors opened. My heart went through the floor when a man in a dark suit emerged, but his features were unfamiliar nor did he indicate the slightest interest in me. Somewhat shaken, I occupied the lift and attempted to map out my explanation to Portney on the journey down. As I stepped out on the ground floor, a man in a gray herringbone suit was entering the lobby of the hotel. I stepped back into the lift and headed it upwards again as fast as I could. The man in the lobby did not have a moustache, but I could not fail to recognize that sallow complexion and iron-gray hair. I had known him as Straithway, the bogus solicitor, and now knew that he was D'Arcy. My problem was to get to Wally's rooms before D'Arcy arrived at the same floor. If I had recognized him, surely the hard-bitten experienced embezzler would spot me in a trice. I raced down the hall and knocked at Wally's door anxiously, bursting in when it was opened.

"He's here," I gasped. "I almost ran into him in the lobby."

"Did he . . .?" began Holmes.

"No. I'm sure of that."

"A near thing," said the sleuth.

As Holmes took Gilligan's inventive plug from

the hole, I stood close to him, my ear pressed to the wall. The first thing I heard was a male voice anxiously posing a question.

"Gaye, what's happened?"

The woman's voice sounded quite young. It came to me that we'd spent a lot of time thinking about this lady whom I had never even seen in person.

"Nothing's happened, Hal. Not yet at least."

"What's that mean?"

"I'm afraid something will when you find out why I cabled you."

"Well?"

"I want to go to a party."

"You want to what?"

"Listen to me now. I've been cooped up in this second-rate hotel for days. Doing nothing, seeing nothing. You've been hiding as though there were five murder warrants out for you. What are we afraid of?"

"I've been playing it extra cautious, that's all. We made a big score, Gaye. I just want to make sure we enjoy it."

"You're playing it so cozy, we'll die of old age before you're ready to make a move."

"All right, tell me about this party that's got you steamed."

"It's the Teasdale Ball, no less."

There was a chuckle from D'Arcy, then his dry tone again.

"Gaye, you can't get within two blocks of that shindig. I read a little about it. The P.M. is going to be there, and the place will be knee deep in peelers."

"Why all the police?"

"There's some gang of jewel thieves that's supposed to have the party targeted. Personally, I think it's publicity. Anyways, what would you be doin' there? It's strictly for the toffs."

"Lady Teasdale is a friend of mine."

"I'll bet."

"You'd lose. She was in the Gaities, same time as me. Think I'm kiddin' eh? Take a glim at this, an invitation to Gaye Farraday and escort."

"You are leveling."

"Come on Hal, you always said you was a sport. How's about rubbin' elbows with the P.M. and Baron Holdernesse and the police commissioner. Even Sherlock Holmes will be there."

"Holmes was the 'nosy Parker' that blew the whistle on Weems."

"So?"

"If it hadn't been fer Holmes . . ."

"You're just talking. Once Weems killed that appraiser, the fat was in the fire. It was time to cut and run."

"Maybe so, but Holmes and that Watson are the only ones I'm frightened of."

"Afraid of that nice little doctor that writes the stories?"

"That nice little doctor, indeed. I don't even think he's a medico. He's Holmes' bodyguard."

"Come off it, Hal."

"I just know what happened to four very rough

lads. Your nice little doctor shot 'em to pieces. He could blow the buttons off that coat of yours and not even singe the cloth."

"You're setting up me. Using Holmes and the Watson fellow as an excuse so as not to take me to the Teasdale affair."

"They've both seen me, remember?"

"So dye your hair and wear a beard. I've seen you do it before."

There was a silence and I threw a quick glance at Holmes. The sleuth was listening intently and I realized that D'Arcy's situation would have much to do with the way he planned to wind up this affair.

"Holmes will be there, you say?" said D'Arcy finally.

"Absolutely, Lady Teasdale told me personally when I met her at my beauty salon."

"Holmes, Watson, Brickstone and an army of constables. O.K. Gaye, sure I'm a sport. We'll take in the Teasdale thing. What a story it will make when we get back to Chicago. They're all lookin' for Weems and I'm right under their noses."

"Oh, Hal."

There was another period of silence during which I assume the woman showed her appreciation in the customary manner that females have.

Then I could hear D'Arcy again.

"All right, Gaye, I'll be here tomorrow . . . about seven, O.K.?"

"Sure."

"If anything goes wrong, I'll cable you here at the

hotel."

"What can go wrong?"

"You never know. See you kid."

Holmes inserted Gilligan's improvised stopper into the hole we had been listening through and signalled Gilligan as he did so. Wally crossed to the large window and stood looking out as planned while Gilligan opened the blinds. The machinery that could show the former Gaye Farraday what could go wrong was in gear.

Curiosity had always been a strong trait of the Watsons, and I moved to one side of the window where I could view, unobserved, the beginnings of this elaborately staged drama. Knowing where Styles and his boys were positioned, it was like waiting for the curtain to rise and the characters to spring into action. The man in the dark suit, whom I'd seen previously in the hall, came out of the hotel entrance. I noted Lacy, working on foot with Slippery Styles, shift his position behind a colonnade of the building on the opposite side of the street but thought nothing of it. The man in the dark suit headed east, walking at a rapid rate, and then I was horrified to see Lacy preceding him in the same direction as Slippery Styles ambled behind both of them. The carriage containing Swifty Summers and Fenn assumed motion and slowly headed in the same direction.

Fortunately, I retained control of my voice for I felt like shouting.

"My God, Holmes, they are following the wrong

man."

The sleuth was at my side in an instant and I indicated the man in the dark suit just disappearing around a corner, well accompanied, though he did not know it.

"That's not D'Arcy, for he is wearing gray herringbone. I saw the chap they are tailing, and I tell you he's not our man."

My friend's hair-trigger mind grasped the situation immediately.

"Wally, stay by this window. Try to see where D'Arcy goes and signal us. Slim, you and Watson and I will try to pick up the chase using Portney's carriage."

He was on his way to the door as he spoke, with Gilligan and me trodding on his heels. The hallway outside was empty so D'Arcy was already on his way down. Holmes' long legs got him to the lifts first, and he punched the button impatiently. As is always the case in such situations, the lift seemed to take an interminable time to reach our floor and seconds were like minutes as we crept down to the lobby. We took precautions before leaving the hotel, for D'Arcy could have been right outside waiting for a carriage, but such was not the case. Slim hailed Portney who must have sensed that something was amiss for he had his carriage in front of the hotel in short order. Holmes was gazing upwards at Wallingford's window. As Slim and I hopped inside the carriage, the sleuth climbed alongside of our tophatted driver.

I opened the hatch in the carriage top, sticking my head through it to learn what was happening and perhaps get some orders from Holmes.

"From Wally's gestures, our man has taken a hansom. Make for Edgware Road, Phineas."

The Cartright Hotel was in that section opposite Hyde Park known as Tyburnia, not far from Paddington Station from which Holmes and I had departed on many a case. When we reached Edgware Road, Holmes had Phineas turn right on the theory that our quarry would be more apt to head towards Oxford Street than the area around St. John's Wood. The good luck which had seemed to desert us, now reasserted itself.

"That hansom ahead is what you're after, Mr. 'Olmes. I seen him pull up in front of the hotel and pick up a single passenger."

"If you're sure it's the same one ..." began Holmes.

"Aye, Sir. The horse is a mite distinctive. That's your boy all right."

"Then let's not overtake him Phineas, but tag along at a reasonable distance."

I relayed the good news to Slim. It seemed we were back in business again.

When we reached Oxford Street, the hansom turned left, as did we. There was sufficient traffic so that our presence could not arouse suspicion. I'd the thought that the hansom might swing right on Park Lane, but it continued in a straight line on Oxford Street. It was not long before we passed Baker Street

on our left. It would have been ironic indeed if
D'Arcy's hideout proved to be in our neighborhood.
It seemed reasonable to assume that he was headed
for his rat hole.

Now we were past New Bond Street and bearing
down on Oxford Circus. Our quarry turned right on
Regent Street and then left on Shaftesbury Avenue.
I noted that Portney had dropped back, putting
more distance between the hansom and our carriage.

" 'Tis but a feeling, Mr. 'Olmes, but he might
have spotted us, you know?"

Holmes had to come to a quick decision. "Where
do you feel that he's headed, Phineas?"

"High Holborn, though he could have just stayed
on Oxford Street."

"I agree. Possibly he became suspicious sooner
than you sensed it. Pass him, Phineas and then go
left on Charing Cross Road.

Having cast the dice, Holmes maneuvered himself from the driver's seat and into the carriage. We
all sat well back when we passed the hansom we had
been in pursuit of.

Holmes positioned himself to watch through the
small bullet window in the rear. When we turned
left on Charing Cross Road, the sleuth kept Slim
and me informed.

"Good. He's stayed on Shaftesbury. We'd have
been in a fix if he'd turned right but I didn't think he
was heading towards Trafalgar Square."

Leaning out the carriage window, Holmes had
words for our driver.

"Let's put on some speed, Phineas. Turn right on New Oxford and I'll wager we can pick him up again."

Holmes resumed his seat inside the carriage. "Now if good fortune graces our guesswork, we can light on Mr. D'Arcy's tail again while his suspicions, if any, are allayed."

A short time later there was a knock on the roof of our carriage.

"I've got him, Mr. 'Olmes."

"Lay well back, Phineas," cautioned the sleuth.

We had just passed the Holborn Restaurant* when the hansom carrying D'Arcy turned right on Little Queen Street. At a signal from Holmes, Slim Gilligan slipped from our carriage and hurried to the corner as Portney slowed his mare to a walk. Having turned the corner, Gilligan reappeared and waved us on. When we drew up to the cracksman, he leaned into the carriage window.

"That there 'ansom's come to a stop 'alf-way up the block, Gov."

Holmes was out of the carriage in but a moment with me climbing down after him.

"Cross the intersection, Phineas, and wait for us down the block," said the sleuth to our driver. Slim was already headed down Little Queen Street, and my friend and I made haste to follow him. The hansom was pulling away from in front of one of the old buildings that line both sides of the street and pre-

---

*Watson took young Stamford to luncheon at the Holborn on the day he first met Sherlock Holmes.

date the Great Fire. We crossed to the other side of Little Queen Street and, standing in the shadows, carefully observed the house in question. As we watched a light appeared on the first floor of the otherwise dark building, and we exchanged looks of satisfaction.

"He's come to roost," said Holmes. "Rented a room in a rather strategic area. Charing Cross Station on one side and St. Pancras on the other. If pursued, The Strand is not far off and a good place to get lost in. All right, Slim, I don't think he has any other journey planned, but you stay and keep an eye on the place. Watson and I will take Portney's carriage to Baker Street and send him back with relief men for you."

"No 'urry, Gov," said the placid Gilligan.

"But I shall," replied the sleuth. "Surely Slippery Styles and his lads will have returned to headquarters, and I'm looking forward to hearing their explanations as to what happened to the great tail job that was going to cover D'Arcy like a tent."

18

The Surprise Ball

"Well," I thought to myself, "there's really nothing more that can be done." D'Arcy's hiding place in High Holborn was under constant surveillance. Burlington Bertie, the waterfront brawler and smash and grab man who had changed his ways because of Sherlock Holmes, was watching D'Arcy, along with his brother, Tiny. A somewhat sheepish Slippery Styles and Swifty Summers were with the boys from Limehouse, so D'Arcy had plenty of uninvited and unseen company. The remainder of the Styles group were keeping tabs on Gaye Farraday in case the husband-wife team should entertain a change in plans.

It puzzled me why Holmes made such a point of Lady Teasdale's ball until I realized that D'Arcy might have taken it into his mind to skip at any time with his wife, and there were official problems relative to stopping him. Holmes had, as yet, no proof regarding D'Arcy's association with the late Weems, and he would need plenty to convince the authorities who did not even know of the existence of the second murderer. Lady Teasdale's affair and its appeal to the female D'Arcy was Holmes' bait to keep the conspirator in London and allow the master sleuth to close down on him.

While we had been occupied locating D'Arcy's hiding place, Lady Teasdale had left no stone unturned in the planning of the event which would, she hoped, advance her into the front ranks of the social whirl. The grand ballroom of the Grosvenor Square Hotel was the chosen site, and her ladyship had spared no pains, or money either, to make the locale suitable for the large group that would be in attendance. The Grosvenor was most dignified and sedate, and its ballroom was a little sombre by reason of its oak panelling. This was relieved by the elegance of its furniture and appointments. Lady Teasdale had further dispelled any suggestion of gloom by having soft gray carpeting laid throughout and there was to be a profusion of flowers. She had decided that delicate strains of music would come from an invisible orchestra concealed behind a canopy of palms.

Somehow the name of "The Surprise Ball" had grown, fueled by references in the press that an event of some sort was slated to take place. Interwoven with this was the fairy story of Holmes' creation regarding the French jewel thieves. Many a dignified dowager who would have been shocked if two dogs chose to display a dislike to each other, could hardly suppress excitement and expectations at the prospect of being present when there was an actual attempt to purloin any of the famous gems sure to be adorning necks, ears and fingers at the Surprise Ball. I suspected that the considerable press coverage had been artificially stimulated by Inspector Athelney Jones' revelations to reporters, said material being authored by Holmes or Wallingford. I was to be present along with the American. Since the plan called for Holmes to be elsewhere, Wally was deputized to spread the rumor that the great detective was on the premises in disguise. It was my fervent hope that a dignified member of Parliament would not get his beard pulled by some audacious young lady obsessed with the idea of revealing the master sleuth incognito.

Now, at last, the great evening was upon us, much to the disgust of the Duchess of Paisley and Lady Windermere, who were significant by their absence. If one were up on that sort of thing, and I was not, he surely would have said that the festivities got off to a good start and continued in that vein. I tried to circulate in the prescribed manner and was surprised at the number of persons who spoke to me without introduction. Their words, as I might have expected, had a sameness.

"Where is Sherlock Holmes?"

It dawned on me that despite the prestigious guests of honor, the sleuth was a main drawing card, not only because of his fame but because he was hardly ever seen socially. By nature my friend was somewhat of a recluse, and while many present were familiar with the drawings of him occasionally seen in the journals, few had actually met him.

Lord Bellinger, the Prime Minister, made an early appearance and caused the expected stir. He promptly buttonholed me with the standard question.

"Your Lordship, Holmes might be here in some sort of disguise, but I suspect that he is not, as yet that is."

"Naturally, he's up to something." The Prime Minister's statement was meant as a question since it embodied the implied "Else what am I doing here?"

"Very much so. Has to do with the people's faith in the financial establishment, you know."

The P.M. didn't know this nor did I, really, but Wallingford had said that I had an honest face.

"Ah, yes," stated Bellinger. "Well, in case I don't get the chance to see Holmes, will you inform him how delighted I am to play an active role, whatever it is, in one of his exploits? I know that he is always conscious of the public good."

Bellinger was right there. Holmes was strongly patriotic and much dedicated to the "Rule Brittania" theme. As suitable in his position, Bellinger made the rounds with his escort of two rather supercilious gentlemen who merely mumbled their names. Then, dedicated to Queen and country, he withdrew, as was customary. It would have excited comment had he not.

Au contraire, Lord Cantlemere and Baron Holdernesse not only arrived in good time but stayed as

long as most. Cantlemere, a widower for many
years, was squiring Mrs. Farintosh, whose opal ti-
ara Holmes had recovered in an early case. The lady
was well known as a sprightly widow and it occurred to me that Cantlemere's presence need not be
attributed solely to my friend's message. As for Holdernesse, the Duchess was with him, and it was the
first time I had ever met the wife of the richest man
in England. When Holmes and I had been involved
in the Baron's difficulties, his marriage was in peril
and the Duchess in the south of France. There was
gratitude in the gaze of the red bearded nobleman
when he introduced me to her and, singularly, he did
not inquire as to Holmes' presence. He had been
asked by the sleuth to attend and that was sufficient.
The Holdernesse family traced their origin and title
back to the Norman Conquest and, in the Middle
Ages, were known as the Marauding Barons of Holdernesse, but their feelings relative to loyalties could
never be questioned.

As for Cecil Brickstone, I had expected him to be
present when the doors of the Grosvenor Square
ballroom opened. Holmes, according to plan, had
suggested to the commissioner that he would provide
a solution to the death of Weems. Even without this
prize apple, Brickstone had every reason for being
present from a political standpoint. There had been
those in his position who had chosen to ignore the
social limelight, but Brickstone was not of that persuasion. Whether this was due to his recent assumption of duties or a secret insecurity, the commission-

er was much committed to the hearty good fellow and handshake approach, as I have already indicated. Also, there was that contagious myth of the jewel thieves, a bit of pure balderdash that seemed to have hoodwinked everyone.

When the commissioner did appear in the first half hour, I assumed that he had been checking precautions outside the hotel, for there were a number of London's finest in the area. This was confirmed by the presence of Quale, the commissioner's assistant. Upon entry, Quale was busy whispering in Brickstone's ear, and the commissioner's eyes were darting to certain portions of the room as he did so.

The professional waiters, hand picked, had the correct clerical air, half complacent, half dignified. Brickstone's attention was directed to others whose attire did not fit them all that well. Nor did they perform their duties with that automatic ease of much practice. The commissioner had the affair, as D'Arcy had prophesied to his wife, "kneedeep in peelers." I tried to negotiate my movements so as to avoid Brickstone, knowing that he would have a bundle of questions to which I had no answers. In this regard, my lucky star shone upon me. Every time the commissioner spotted me and made a purposeful move in my direction, someone spoke to him, and the politician in him would not allow a short answer.

Then the tables were filled and the guests did the same with a continuous replenishing of glasses. As to the problems of who sat next to whom and the mysteries of social in-fighting, I know not, but I can attest to the quality of the liquid refreshments which had to prove satisfactory to the most critical of vintage experts. It crossed my mind that future inventories of the late Sir Basil Teasdale's famous wine cellar would take less time. Our hostess was, as the saying goes, going "all out" and garnering top grades in the going.

Then the dancing began. By this time I had lost track of our hostess and Wallingford as well. I had been trying to get with the American for a private moment since, though I tried desperately not to appear obvious, my eyes kept returning to Gaye Farraday and her escort. This gentleman was the focal point of the whole evening as far as we were concerned, and he had me bemused. Physically, he could have been D'Arcy, being tall and of the same contours. However, he certainly didn't look like the man as I remembered from my last brief glimpse of him entering the lobby of the Cartright Hotel. His hair was quite long and he had prominent sideburns. The pronounced sallow complexion was not in evidence but all of that could have been the product of disguise. Holmes did not have a corner on the art of cosmetic deception. I was sure that I would not have spotted him had he not been with Gaye Farraday, which bothered me. The whole idea was to have D'Arcy accounted for while Holmes ransacked his hideaway for the necessary evidence.

A set came to an end and, as the dancers returned to their seats, there was a drumroll and a flourish from a single trumpet. Lady Teasdale stood on the stairs leading down to the ballroom, obviously gathering eyes.

"Hello, what's this?" I thought. "Something worked out between Holmes and her ladyship, perhaps?" I never did learn the answer to that.

"Ladies and gentlemen . . ." she began and then paused as a silence settled over the ballroom. Having had some experience with audiences, she waited until she had everyone's attention and then began again.

"Ladies and gentlemen, I trust that you are enjoying yourselves."

This prompted an enthusiastic round of applause, which her ladyship attempted to bring to a conclusion with outstretched palm, though I knew it was a symphony to her ears.

"Thank you, and my thanks to you all for being here. Now I have a confession to make. Somehow this affair in honor of my late husband has gained the name of 'The Surprise Ball.' I really don't know how this came about but that is unimportant since we can't have any of you disappointed. So we shall have a surprise, and it is as much a mystery to me as to you. Our surprise has been placed in the hands of one very familiar with mystery, Mr. Sherlock Holmes."

There was an undercurrent of whispered comments and an interchange of glances at this statement, and her ladyship certainly had an attentive audience.

"Would Mr. Holmes kindly step forward and surprise us?" she asked.

"Well," I thought, "Holmes has certainly done it this time. He promised Brickstone a solution, and he's going to do it with an introduction and audience as well. The proceedings had a touch of the flamboyant far removed from one of Holmes' quiet unravelings."

There was a lengthy pause during which absolutely nothing happened. It became uncomfortable and I sensed that a nervous titter was near at hand. Her ladyship must have felt this as well, for she took the only course possible and dealt me one of the biggest surprises of my life.

"Since Mr. Holmes may not be present at the moment, may I ask his intimate friend and biographer, Dr. John Watson, to take charge?"

There was scattered applause as, dumbfounded, I mounted the stairs to stand beside her ladyship. Before I could think of a comment, Lady Teasdale, with a graceful gesture, stepped aside and there I stood, the center of all eyes. I was totally unprepared for this turn of events and had not the slightest idea of what I was supposed to say. Was this nightmare some part of Holmes' confidence game that no one had thought to tell me about? Where, by all the saints in heaven, was Sherlock Holmes?

Possibly prompted by the idea of a confidence game, there came to my mind a frequent remark of Wallingford: "When in doubt, fake it." Having no choice, fake it I did.

"Ladies and gentlemen, for the past two weeks our journals have made much of the death of an appraiser named James Wyndhaven. As you all know by now, Sherlock Holmes solved this matter with the assistance of Commissioner Brickstone who is here with us tonight."

An inspiration caused me to gesture towards where Brickstone was sitting, a move which prompted applause from the gathering and also stimulated Brickstone to rise and bow. Anything, anything to keep the ball rolling until somehow I was rescued from this impossible situation.

"However, the death of Wyndhaven became an even more baffling affair for I can now relate to you something which you did not read with your morning coffee or in the early evening editions."

There was a complete hush and I could afford to speak in measured tones, having everyone caught up with the thought of being among the first to know. Believe me, I did speak slowly, for I was prolonging the moments as much as I could.

"It was the fugitive, Geoffrey Weems, who murdered James Wyndhaven, but Weems himself has been murdered."

Exclamations of surprise greeted this, and I waited till they died down, fervently wishing that they wouldn't.

"Weems was a co-conspirator in a plot to embezzle funds from the firm of Leicester Ltd. in which he was employed. I should state that the funds have been recovered through the efforts of Mr. Holmes, and there is no question as to the stability, nay, affluence, of the investment house."

I was certain that my last remark would save Frontnoy Leicester, our client, from heart failure.

"Weems was killed by his partner in crime, the motive being the familiar one of greed. Having, from time to time, assumed the role of an author in bringing some of Mr. Holmes' cases to print . . ."

Here I paused, hoping for some applause, but none came.

" . . . I am struck by the very unusual aspect of this case. A murderer who, in turn, is murdered. As you may, by now, have guessed, your surprise tonight is the final solution to this chain of events. Among the guests this evening is the woman who is married to the late Weems' fellow conspirator. I would like the former Miss Gaye Farraday and her companion to rise."

There was no more for me to say, really. I had to be rescued now for I had reached the end of my rope.

Relief came, but not from the source anticipated.

Brickstone was on his feet and a number of burly pseudo-waiters were surveying the crowd with suspicious looks. As if in a trance, Gaye Farraday had come to her feet and the man with her as well. It was he who burst our vehemently.

"Look 'ere, I brought Gaye to this party, but don't go figuring me fer a murderer. I'm an understudy in the Vanities at the Park Row Theatre. Gaye got stood up fer the evenin' and asked me to give 'er a 'and, which I did. Anybody at the Vanities will tell

yuh me name's 'arry Saunders, and I never murdered anybody in me life. I'm innocent you 'ear."

"Indeed you are, Mr. Saunders."

Those were the sweetest words I'd ever heard, for
I could certainly recognize the calm and authoritative tone of Sherlock Holmes.

There he stood, at the head of the stairs. Slightly
behind him was Burlington Bertie and his brother,
Tiny, a mere two hundred and eighty pounds of
bone and muscle. Between then was a bedraggled
figure which I immediately recognized as D'Arcy,
while Inspector Jones brought up the rear.

Everyone in the room knew — or sensed — who
was speaking now.

"Behind me is Holbrook D'Arcy, a known swindler, who murdered his partner Geoffrey Weems.
While his wife was attending this gala, D'Arcy
planned to leave for parts unknown with the proceeds of the Leicester theft. Fortunately, I am able to
pass him over to our Commissioner of Police along
with proof of his guilt."

Gaye Farraday's beauty was destroyed by the raw
look of rage, and she was screaming invectives at
D'Arcy as policemen moved in on her. Brickstone
had rushed forward and was beside me as Holmes
joined us quickly.

"Commissioner, keep the wife and husband separated. I'm sure she is ready to tell you the whole
story. Jones and the boys also have a few items of
interest."

As Brickstone signalled his men and Gaye Farraday and D'Arcy were spirited away, the gathering burst into a babble of sound, many wondering if all of this had really happened. They had been observers of the windup of a much discussed mystery and were having some difficulty in believing it.

Lady Teasdale's Surprise Ball was also much discussed, and for days and months to come. Holmes had kept his word to her ladyship and, for those interested in such things, the winter social season of London had gotten off to a very auspicious beginning.

19

The Oldest Con in the Game

"It came to my mind, Watson, while we were eavesdropping on D'Arcy and his wife. He made such a point of the fact that everyone of interest to him would be at the same place at the same time. I could almost see the wheels of his mind turning. You and I and a considerable segment of the metropolitan police force accounted for and his wife as well. A perfect time for him to depart with all of the proceeds of his elaborate scheme. Being certain that he would not appear at the Surprise Ball gave us an advantage. No search for the funds acquired from Manheim's securities. D'Arcy had them with him when we grabbed him, of course. Then there was the turning of wife against husband. Gaye Farraday will take relish in revealing everything to Brickstone. Also, the matter of accessories of Weems' and labels from his suit, removed to prevent identification. D'Arcy hadn't disposed of them as yet. It all adds up to a perfect case for the Crown against the fellow."

"But Holmes, if you had any idea of what I went through. . . :"

"Now that I must apologize for, old chap. Our timing was a mite awry but, from reports, you carried off the whole matter splendidly. Truly in the style of 'Holmes' bodyguard,' to quote D'Arcy."

This stifled my complaints for I well knew the sleuth would not let me forget that title foisted on me.

We were at breakfast the following morning with an unusually bright sun bathing our sitting room with light and warmth. Holmes was a rapid eater and finished before me. Rather than enjoy a morning cigarette, as was his custom, he took himself to the desk, securing paper and envelope. Pen in hand, he looked at me and sighed.

"Now for the accounting, for I have in mind a trip to Leicester Ltd. to confer with our client."

This surprised me for the finances of our cases were usually taken care of in our quarters. However, there were other thoughts uppermost in my mind.

"You're thinking of the fee, of course. I trust that you will make it a sizable one. The expenses associated with this matter were considerable."

"Yes," he agreed, "we must keep in mind a bonus for the lads though Slippery Styles may try to refuse his."

"Oh, the matter of following D'Arcy," I replied with a chuckle.

"Slippery hasn't stopped blaming himself for that, but we shall remind him that it was his discovering the existence of Gaye Farraday that gave us the vital clue, Watson." The sleuth mused for a moment, gazed at the ceiling, and then penned some short sentences on stationery, folded it and placed it in an envelope which he addressed to Frontnoy Leicester.

I had hurried through the rest of my breakfast and risen to observe his actions for reasons known only to myself.

Billy, the page boy, made an appearance at this time with a cablegram for Holmes. My friend read the message with, it seemed to me, satisfaction, but he made no reference to it as he placed it in his coat pocket.

"Well, Watson, shall we ready ourselves for our final journey relative to this quite unusual affair?" he asked.

We did and, while Holmes was otherwise occupied, I succeeded in getting to the desk, for there was a little paper work that I wished to do.

When we arrived at the Savage Building in the late morning and made our way to the eighth floor offices of the investment house, Mabel Stark, the receptionist, made her employer aware of our presence through the switchboard phone.

After disconnecting, her direct gaze crossed swords with Holmes'.

"Mr. Leicester will be with you in a moment, gentlemen."

I could understand this. The financier was probably girding himself to receive the news of what the sleuth's carte blanche fee would be.

The delay did not nettle Holmes. Indeed, he welcomed it for, as mentioned, he did fancy tying off loose threads.

"Miss Stark, several days back Inspector Athelney Jones came here with a fellow officer from the Yard in hopes of finding Geoffrey Weems."

"That's right, Mr. Holmes. However, Mr. Weems was not in the office, and I told the police I did not know where he was at the moment. The inspector requested the use of a phone and I let him into the visitor's office and placed a call to Scotland Yard for him. After that, Inspector Jones and his associate asked some questions of the staff and remained here until closing time." The receptionist's voice was flat. She might have been telling Holmes the time of day.

As he just stared at her, she registered a slight impatience.

"That's the way it happened."

"Not quite," responded the sleuth. "Weems was not here, but you knew where he was. On a client call or doing some research work, probably. When the opportunity presented itself, you called Weems and notified him that two men from Scotland Yard were at the office waiting for him to appear. Inasmuch as this happened after my questioning of Weems, he was able to draw a conclusion, and that is how he got the jump on the authorities and made his way to his partner's hideout in High Holborn."

"I had no way of knowing he was going to do that, Mr. Holmes. I always found Mr. Weems a pleasant man." Defiance crept into the woman's manner. "If we could roll back the hours and days, I would do the same thing over again. You can include that in your report to Scotland Yard, Mr. Holmes."

"I don't intend to make one. The consequences are something you will have to face in your own mind. Had you not alerted Weems, giving him the chance to escape, he would not have ended up in the Gravesend morgue."

There were two tears forming in this unemotional woman's eyes as the door to Leicester's private office opened and he invited us to join him.

The financier's self-discipline had erected a stoic mask to cover his feelings, but there was the sense of nervous expectation about him as he ushered us to chairs and resumed his customary position behind his large desk.

"Well, Mr. Holmes, this matter seems to have finally come to a conclusion."

"You find it a satisfactory one, I believe?"

Leicester had reservations regarding this. "The funds secured through the sale of Herr Manheim's stolen securities have been returned to me." The man approached his next point with seeming re-grets. "Our arrangement was that you would at-tempt to cover up the matter of the stolen securities."

"I have done so. As far as the public is concerned, Weems and D'Arcy embezzled funds from your organization. Nothing more specific than that."

"But D'Arcy will go on trial."

"For the murder of Weems. The Prosecutor for the Crown will not introduce the matter of Manheim's securities. He has no reason to."

"But the defense, Mr. Holmes?"

"D'Arcy's legal representative will avoid that subject like a plague. As long as a general term like funds is used, D'Arcy is a partner with Weems in the theft. If the matter of Manheim's securities and their replacement with stolen stocks and bonds, secured from underworld connections, is brought up, then D'Arcy becomes the mastermind of the scheme and appears in even a worse light."

The financier was regarding Holmes with a touch of disbelief.

"I didn't really think you could do it."

"I believe you did express doubt," replied the sleuth, and his manner was somewhat curt. "There is one additional matter that has not been touched upon. This entire affair revolved around Herr Manheim's securities. Has there been any report made to him relative to his portfolio?"

With both elbows on his desk, Leicester's head sank into outstretched hands as if to erase this question from his mind.

"I was so worried about other matters, I just couldn't face it," he admitted.

"I did," said Holmes. "I sent him a detailed report. Just prior to coming here, I received a cablegram from Berlin which should prove of interest to you." My friend had secured the cable form from his pocket and read from it.

"Your message appreciated. No concern from this end since you stipulate you will represent my best interests in this matter. Manheim."

"You mean he's not going to raise a fuss about this?" asked Leicester.

"Not when I assure him that his portfolio is as it was in every respect."

The financier nodded eagerly. "I can guarantee that and within twenty-four hours it will be an accomplished fact."

"Then I believe our arrangements are, indeed, concluded," said Holmes. He extracted the envelope from his pocket, a move that I had been waiting for.

"Here, Holmes," I said, coming to my feet. "Allow me." I took the envelope from his hand and turned to cross to Leicester's desk.

"Dr. Watson handles much of our business," stated the sleuth as I laid an envelope in front of the financier.

Leicester slit it open quickly to extract the enclosed sheet which he viewed. Then consternation spread over his features.

"Mr. Holmes . . . this fee . . ."

"Of my choosing . . ." interjected the sleuth.

"But it is without precedence. Such a sum . . ."

"One moment," said my friend in a steely voice. "Your problems solved, you are now haggling over this matter? May I remind you that talents less than mine receive ten percent of returned stolen goods without question."

"But this amount . . ." stuttered Leicester. Then with his jaw clenched, he extracted his checkbook from a drawer and filled out a check with shaky fingers. Inasmuch as I was standing beside him, he handed it to me.

"There is your fee, Mr. Holmes, but I am giving it to you under protest."

"Come Watson," replied Holmes, bounding to his feet. His patience, never as strong as the village blacksmith, seemed to have given out. "We must leave, for I have a feeling we are in Piccadilly surrounded by fruit carts and vendors."

Making for the door indignantly, with me on his heels, Holmes suddenly turned and leveled an outstretched finger at Leicester as I barely avoided bumping into him.

"When you have carefully considered this matter, Sir, I believe you will realize that you have received full value for every pence you have paid. When you do, I shall expect an apology."

The financier was also on his feet. "I must warn you, Mr. Holmes, that I very seldom apologize for anything."

"Then time will decide," said Holmes as we departed.

In a hansom returning to Baker Street, my friend was a far cry from the calm and cool theorist.

"Can you imagine the gall of the man? Attempting to barter like a common fishmonger."

"What fee did you ask for, Holmes?"

"You saw the check, Watson, and have it in your pocket."

I backtracked desperately. "I mean, what decided you on the sum?"

"It occurred to me that we were involved in another case with some points of similarity. Recall that the Duke of Holdernesse offered us six thousand pounds apiece if we could return Lord Saltire and suppress the matter of his disappearance."

"An offer that you refused," was my response.

"But the sum stuck in my mind. Considering the important matters involved in this affair, I charged Leicester six thousand pounds, as you know."

"Not until this moment, Holmes. It has been my contention that you consistently undervalue your talents, and your real reward is the game and not the gain."

"Ah, we're back to that again," replied the sleuth, looking at me quizzically.

"Besides, there are all the expenses involved which I have mentioned. Also the fact that I plan to resume business arrangements with certain bookmakers as well as my Tuesday and Thursday afternoons of billiards at Thurstons. That is why, at the earliest convenience, I'm going to the City and Suburban and deposit Leicester's check for twenty thousand pounds."

"What?" exclaimed Holmes, his eyes wide with astonishment.

"It's the oldest con in the game, Holmes. The old envelope switch, and I had an expert teacher."

"You and Wallingford dreamed this up."

"No. Wally but taught me the skill. The idea was mine."

Slowly shock faded from Holmes' face and then the ends of his lips twitched.

"Twenty thousand pounds. No wonder the old chap seemed about to have a stroke."

"He paid it. Furthermore, I'll wager that you will receive your apology."

"You can't be serious?"

"I'm one hundred pounds serious."

"Watson, as you know, I'm not a gambling man. However, in this instance I will make an exception."

We shook hands on it.

It was fully two months later, and I had decided that I should, in all honesty, pay Holmes his one hundred pounds. How long does it take a man to make up his mind, even a stubborn old horsethief like Leicester? I was actually rummaging for my checkbook when Billy delivered the morning mail.

Holmes was busy with an experiment in his chemical corner so I sorted out the envelopes, one of which gave me pause.

"I say, Holmes, here is a puzzler."

"In what way, old chap?"

I displayed the envelope. "Addressed to you. In the upper left-hand corner, three words are imprinted. 'The Leicester Letter.' "

Holmes extinguished the gas jet under a vessel of liquid and began toweling off his hands.

"Oh, yes. That annual or semi-annual advice that

has such an effect on the world of finance. Possibly our former client has given us a gift subscription to his words of wisdom. Do open it, old chap, and see what moves the grand old man of the exchange advocates."

I did and regarded the single page within. "He is sparing with words."

"We were informed that was his style. What does he say?"

"Avoid cotton futures during this period."

"I guess we can do that."

"That's not all. 'Buy Falmouth Industries on price dips.'"

"Two utterances from the oracle."

"Actually, there are three, Holmes. The last reads as follows: 'Not relative to commodity or investment dealings. When in doubt, contact Sherlock Holmes.'"

The sleuth regarded me blankly for a moment and then burst out with as good a laugh as I had heard him enjoy in some time.

"I do believe that is the most subtle apology I've ever received," he stated. "Also, it serves as a cue for a windfall of one hundred pounds to come to you, good fellow."

Holmes sat right down and made me out a check for that amount.

One week later I lost the entire sum when my sure winner in the Wessex Cup broke badly, was bumped at the first turn and finished a poor fourth.

Oh well, easy come, easy go.